"I can't keep my hands off you," he said, his voice close to a whisper.

She looked down at their intertwined fingers and watched him raise her hand to his mouth and kiss it. Her stomach fluttered. He stepped closer and kissed her forehead. Tayler placed her head against his hard chest as he wrapped his arms around her. *I'm so weak for this man.* She begged for strength.

"Rollin, we can't do this again."

"Can't do what? We can't dance?" he asked in a soft, controlled voice. His body swayed with the music and she found herself following his lead. He shifted and his thigh pressed between her legs, and her thigh did the same. They slow danced in the middle of the library.

He ignited a fire inside Tayler that intensified when he reached down and placed his hand under her chin, bringing her face up to meet his. He kissed her lips ever so gently and Tayler closed her eyes. Her head told her to pull away from his embrace before it was too late, but her body had a mind of its own and wanted nothing more than to revel in his embrace.

Dear Reader,

I hope you enjoy reading *When I Fall in Love* as much as I enjoyed writing it. Coleman House came to me while riding through the country in Kentucky and seeing this massive house that reminded me of Tara from *Gone with the Wind*. My curiosity about who lived there took over. My own experience at a B and B fueled the rest. I have too many ideas for just one book, so watch out for book number two!

To find out about future releases and learn more about me and my past releases, you can sign up for my newsletter on my website at www.bridgetanderson.net. I love to connect with readers, so follow me on Twitter, @banders319, or Facebook.com/banders319. I appreciate all reviews. Please leave one on your retailer's site or on Goodreads to help other readers discover my novels.

Thank you,

Bridget Anderson

WHEN I FALL IN Love

Bridget Anderson

 HARLEQUIN® KIMANI™ ROMANCE

If you purchased this book without a cover you should be aware that this book is stolen property. It was reported as "unsold and destroyed" to the publisher, and neither the author nor the publisher has received any payment for this "stripped book."

Recycling programs for this product may not exist in your area.

ISBN-13: 978-0-373-86449-2

When I Fall in Love

Copyright © 2016 by Bridget Anderson

All rights reserved. The reproduction, transmission or utilization of this work in whole or in part in any form by any electronic, mechanical or other means, now known or hereinafter invented, including xerography, photocopying and recording, or in any information storage or retrieval system, is forbidden without written permission. For permission please contact Harlequin Kimani, 225 Duncan Mill Road, Toronto, Ontario M3B 3K9, Canada.

This is a work of fiction. Names, characters, places and incidents are either the product of the author's imagination or are used fictitiously, and any resemblance to actual persons, living or dead, business establishments, events or locales is entirely coincidental.

® and TM are trademarks of Harlequin Enterprises Limited or its corporate affiliates. Trademarks indicated with ® are registered in the United States Patent and Trademark Office, the Canadian Intellectual Property Office and in other countries.

For questions and comments about the quality of this book please contact us at CustomerService@Harlequin.com.

HARLEQUIN®
www.Harlequin.com

Printed in U.S.A.

Bridget Anderson is a native of Louisville, Kentucky. She currently resides in North Metro Atlanta with her husband and their big dog who she swears is part human. She's published seven novels and two novellas. Her romance suspense novel, *Rendezvous*, was adapted into a made-for-television movie. She is a member of Romance Writers of America, Georgia Romance Writers and The Authors Guild.

Bridget writes provocative romance stories about smart women and the men they love. When she's not writing, she loves to travel. She's fallen in love with Paris, France, and can't wait to get back to Ghana, West Africa.

Books by Bridget Anderson

Harlequin Kimani Romance

When I Fall in Love

This one's for my critique partner, Shirley Harrison,
who helped me discover NaNoWriMo
and get my writing legs back.

Also, for my family and friends who constantly ask,
"When's the next novel?"

Chapter 1

"Okay, I exited the expressway thirty minutes ago and I'm still not seeing anything but trees, fields and fields of grass, and a bunch of cows. So, where in the hell is this place?" With both hands on the steering wheel, Tayler Carter yelled at her girlfriend Nicole through her car's speakers using the Bluetooth feature.

"What exit did you take?"

"The Blue Belt Grassway, highway, or something like that, and I've only seen three cars in the last half hour. What is this, the road to nowhere?" The scenic drive was making Tayler's bottom numb.

"Girl, I told you your GPS was going to go out on that road. Where are the directions I emailed you?"

Tayler shrugged and rolled her eyes, thankful Nicole couldn't see her. She reached over for a piece of paper in the driver's seat. "I've got my Mapquest directions."

"Mapquest! I told you to use the directions I sent you. There's a new road that isn't on Mapquest. Maybe your GPS will pick up in a little while. Try it again."

"Dammit." Tayler let out a heavy sigh and eased her foot up off the gas pedal.

"Don't worry, I'll talk you in."

"No, that's not it," she said, glancing in the rearview mirror. "I finally see another car on this freakin' road and it's a police car flashing his lights at me. How did I get so damn lucky?"

"Oh, yeah, I forgot to tell you the police are pretty heavy down there."

"How come I have a feeling there's a lot you've forgotten to tell me?"

"How fast were you going?"

"Let's just say I doubt he'll be satisfied with a warning."

"Want me to hang on the line while you pull over?"

"No, I've got this. I'll call you back later."

Fifteen minutes later, white picket fences with large homes that sat back off the main road finally came into view. But only to be replaced seconds later by smaller houses with swings or rocking chairs on the front porches. As Tayler drove through what must have been downtown Danville, Kentucky, several people either waved or stared as she passed. They all seemed to have the one thing she didn't have—family. She drove by the post office, several small churches and a few local stores as she followed her police escort, and then they swung a right, heading away from town. Soon they were back to white picket fences and another two-lane road.

She was accustomed to traveling alone, but had to admit to a touch of fear as her police escort carried her farther away from the town. The road had lots of twists and turns before opening up to lush fields of green farmland that took her breath away. The police car turned off the main road onto another country road.

She breathed a sigh of relief when she saw a large white sign with black letters reading Coleman House Bed-and-Breakfast.

Here at last.

The officer slowed and let her pull her BMW to a stop beside him. She lowered her window. In his dark shades he sort of reminded her of actor Jake Gyllenhaal.

"Just keep on this road," he said in his local dialect. "The farm's a couple yards down the way."

"Thank you. I appreciate this."

"No problem. Be sure and tell Rollin Greg said hello."

She waved. "I'll be sure to do that."

The police car turned around and spun back out onto the road. She continued down a long oak tree–lined path, which yielded to another sign—Coleman Organic Farm. *So I really am in the country, on a farm and all*, she thought. She turned off the air conditioner and lowered the windows. She wanted to smell the country. Did it really smell like cows and pigs, or grass and fresh air? In her thirty-six years she'd never been to the country. She preferred the city with all its modern conveniences. This vacation was going to be an experience she knew she'd never forget.

The road curved and the oak trees ended. Ahead of her sat a miniature version of Tara, the mansion from

Gone With the Wind, one of her favorite romantic movies. The house had the same four white columns on the porch and gave off a grand appearance. A warm, fuzzy feeling consumed her and put a smile on her face. She pulled her car into one of the parking spaces in front and looked up at the house as if a footman would be exiting any minute to help her with her luggage.

Laughing to herself, she opened the car door and stepped out, stretching out her arms. After a seven-hour drive, she was ready for a good meal and a soft bed. Her Jimmy Choo platform heels might have been perfect for helping her five-three frame reach the gas pedal, but they quickly sank into the gravel driveway, risking scuffs. She reached back into the car and pulled a tube of peppermint lip gloss from her purse and applied some before licking her lips. She adjusted her sunglasses and closed the car door. Pulling her suitcase from the trunk and rolling it through the gravel to the blacktop leading to the house was no easy task. She stopped to take in the view once more. The place was magnificent. In the distance she saw a man sitting on a tractor in the middle of the field. *Just like something out of a Norman Rockwell painting*, she thought.

The front door swung open as she moved her suitcase up the handicapped ramp.

"Welcome to Coleman House Bed and Breakfast. You must be Tayler Carter."

Surprised to be greeted by an older man in a pair of overalls holding a large pitcher of something, Tayler stopped and removed her sunglasses.

"Yes, I am."

"Come on in. She's been expecting you."

She? Tayler had thought Nicole's cousin was a man.

She pulled her suitcase across the front porch past two large white rocking chairs.

The man juggled the pitcher in his hand and reached for her suitcase. "Let me get that for you. Would you like a glass of lemonade?"

"No thank you."

She stepped inside, expecting a grand foyer like the one at Tara.

"You can just step over to the counter there." He nodded to a small area to the right of the staircase. "My wife will get you all settled in. I'll be right back."

He left her suitcase at the foot of the stairs and disappeared down the hall.

Was that Rollin, she wondered.

Tayler did a 360, taking in the custom drapes, the wide spiral staircase and the antique furniture scattered about. The house had an intimate look and feel to it.

"Well, you must be Tayler."

A middle-aged woman walked up to Tayler, wiping her hands off on a kitchen towel, and then extended her hand.

"I'm at a disadvantage here. Seems like everybody knows me." Tayler accepted the woman's hand.

"I'm Rita, the housekeeper, and that lug back there is my husband, Wallace. He'll be up directly to take your suitcase to your room. Nicole told us to expect you. I'm supposed to check you in." She walked behind the registration desk and looked around as though she wasn't quite sure what to do.

"It's nice to meet you, Rita."

"Yes, ma'am, we'll just get you to sign the book here. And I don't rightly know where the receipt book is, so why don't I let Rollin handle that." She handed Tayler a pen.

Tayler smiled. They actually had guest sign in, like something out of an old movie. How quaint—or antiquated, she wasn't sure which. The minute she finished signing the book, Wallace returned and scooped up her suitcase.

"You're in the first room up there on the left." Rita pointed up the stairs. "It faces the fields and you'll get good sunlight in the morning. Did you have much trouble finding the place?" she asked as she came from behind the counter and motioned for Tayler to follow her husband up the stairs.

"A little, but I was fortunate enough to get a police escort."

"Really, from who? Tim?"

"No, he said his name was Greg." Tayler held onto the banister as her heels sank into the plush carpet on the stairs. Everything was polished to a high gloss shine and smelled like fresh lemons.

"Oh, yeah, that's Greg Mason. He's a nice enough fella. He went to high school with Rollin."

"Here you go, ladies. I'll be out back if you need me." Wallace set her suitcase inside the door and backed out.

"In here is your bathroom." Rita gave Tayler a quick tour of her room and then the rest of the second floor. There were three other bedrooms, two of which were occupied. After the tour, she instructed Tayler to return to the lobby after she'd freshened up and Rollin would complete her check-in.

Tayler dropped her purse on the bed and looked around the room with all its ruffles and flowers. If she'd had her own room growing up she would have wanted something with ruffles. But now that style was too country for her taste. But country or not, it would be her home for the next two months.

Rollin switched off the tractor and climbed down. He walked across the yard to the barn, thinking about the pair of legs that had just climbed out of a sports car and walked into his house. She had to be his cousin Nicole's friend from Chicago.

"So, how the fields lookin' this afternoon?"

Rollin turned around to find his uncle Wallace walking into the barn with both hands in the pockets of his overalls.

"Everything's cool. What's up? You ready to stop working on them broke-down cars and join me?"

Wallace laughed and greeted his nephew with a handshake and a hug.

Every time Wallace dropped by, Rollin messed with him about being a mechanic instead of joining him on the farm. Wallace had never wanted to own a farm like Rollin's father, Rollin Joe Sr. Instead, Wallace, a wizard with cars, had opened his first auto body shop fifteen years ago.

"Boy, you know I don't know nothin' 'bout no farming. I'll stick to cars, if you don't mind. Hey, you got a guest up at the house, and Rita don't know how to check her in. She told her you'd be up directly, to help."

"Yeah, I'm on my way up." He knocked the dust off his jeans and pulled his T-shirt over his head. He quickly grabbed another T-shirt from a peg and pulled it on. "I don't know why I agreed to let Nicole's friend stay so long. I'm thinking about closing down the B and B."

"You did it because Nicole's family and this woman is a good friend of hers. Besides, I don't think you'll be regretting anything once you get up to the house."

Rollin glanced back at the lopsided grin on his uncle's face and shook his head. Wallace was what he called an old player, one who'd finally settled down with his third wife.

After freshening up a bit, Tayler grabbed her purse and headed downstairs. The second floor was still quiet and she wondered where the other guests were. On her descent she heard a deep male voice that sent a slight shiver down her spine. The velvety-smooth voice grew louder as she came closer to the first floor. The front door stood wide-open and standing in its midst was a fine, tall piece of sculptured art. The man had on nice-fitting jeans, work boots and a black T-shirt that hugged every muscular inch of his upper body.

He turned from the door and his gaze slowly traveled up the stairs, almost knocking Tayler on her butt. She gripped the banister to keep from tumbling down face-first. A pair of beautiful almond-shaped brown eyes stared up at her.

Oh, my God. Is that Rollin?

Chapter 2

The man's lips moved, but Tayler didn't hear a word coming out of his mouth. He licked his lips before the corners of his mouth turned up into a smile, enticing her with those dimples. A well-groomed mustache and sexy goatee completed his manly look. She took another step and almost fell, but willed her feet to get her down the rest of the steps without embarrassing her.

He walked over and met her at the foot of the stairs. "You must be Tayler. I'm Rollin Coleman Jr." He extended his hand.

She accepted his firm handshake. "Tayler Carter. It's nice to meet you."

"Just step over here and I'll get you all checked in." He walked over behind the counter.

Tayler followed him, taking full advantage of the view. *Why in the hell is this man working on a farm instead of modeling underwear in a magazine some-where?*

He pulled her name up on the computer. "So, Nicole said you wanted to stay a month. Is that right?"

"A month or two, I had told her. She said to let you know once I arrived." As he worked the computer keys her eyes traveled up his arms, stopping at his biceps, which were speaking to her in a language she wanted to learn.

He arched a brow. "A month or two?"

"Yes. Is that gonna be a problem?"

He took a deep breath and shook his head. "Probably not. This late in August, most of the summer crowd has gone. You must have one hell of a job to get that much vacation time."

"Yeah." She didn't want to talk about her leave or why she wanted to stay two months.

"So, how do you want to pay for this, a week at a time or a month at a time?"

"How about a month?" She handed over her credit card.

"That'll work. Who knows, a month might be all you can take," he said with a sour look on his face.

Tayler furrowed her brows. *What the hell did he mean by that?*

While he finished the transaction, she turned around to admire more of the beautiful foyer and its great crown moldings.

"This is a beautiful house. It reminds me of Tara—"

"From *Gone with the Wind*," they said in unison. She smiled, but he sort of frowned, as if he hated that she had said that.

"Yeah, we get that a lot," Rollin said. "My parents

built the place, but I don't know if they were fans or not." He walked from behind the counter. "Come on, I've got time for a quick tour."

He started on the first floor and walked her through the dining room, where he said meals would be served. He then led her through the living room/library, where walls of books resided and afternoon tea would be served. There was also a small recreation room, with a billiard table and other forms of entertainment like board games and cards.

His private quarters, off-limits to guests, were beyond the staircase across from the kitchen.

She waited until they were outside overlooking the meditation garden to ask about the other guests.

"I don't see any other guests lingering around."

"They're in town at a family reunion."

"How many people are there?"

"Two couples, one from Missouri and another from Georgia."

Everyone was coupled up, she noticed, which made her feel out of place. "And then there's me," she said jokingly.

He glanced over at her. "And then there's you," he said before walking back toward the house.

Tayler stood there with her hands on her hips, speechless. She was merely trying to be funny, but his tone had been sharp. Rollin Coleman was rude. She caught up with him at the front door, which wasn't easy to do in heels.

"Excuse me, but do you have a problem with me being here?"

He stopped and turned around. "No, I don't. Why do you ask?"

"Because I'm getting some really bad vibes from you, and you haven't been exactly hospitable during this *little tour*."

He stopped and took a deep breath, giving Tayler an admiring glance before exhaling. "I'm sorry, you're right. I haven't been very gracious, have I? Long day. Why don't we start over?" He cleared his throat. "Thank you for choosing Coleman House Bed-and-Breakfast. I'm Rollin Coleman Jr."

He held his hand out and displayed the most captivating smile, with adorable dimples. His smile brightened up his face and seemed so warm and genuine. *Not only is he built like a Greek statue, but look at those perfect white teeth.* She quickly excused his previous bad behavior and accepted his hand.

"Nice to meet you, Rollin. I'm Tayler Carter."

"The pleasure's all mine, Ms. Carter. I hope you had a pleasant drive down?"

"I did. Thank you very much." She wanted to laugh at his exaggerated greeting. "By the way, Officer Greg said to tell you hello."

"What did you do? Get a speeding ticket?"

"No, he had mercy on this out-of-towner and escorted me here instead."

"Mighty nice of him. Well, let's go back inside. You'll need to change shoes for the rest of the tour."

Tayler looked down at the platform heels that gave her five-three frame a boost. "Why? They're very comfortable, considering I've been sitting on my ass for the last seven hours." Her feet were tired, but she didn't see the need to tell him that.

"You drove all the way down here in those?" he asked with a dubious look on his face.

She shrugged. "Yes, I did." Heels were a part of her casual attire, but he didn't need to know that.

The front door opened and Rita stuck her head out.

"Rollin, excuse me, but Corra called and said she needs you over at her house. It's an emergency."

He shook his head. "Wonder what she's broken now. Rita, if you don't mind, would you show Ms. Carter around the property?"

"Sure," Rita said as she stepped outside.

"Oh, please, call me Tayler."

Rollin smiled. "Tayler. Got it. Well, I'm sorry I have to leave, but let Rita know if you need anything. I'll see you ladies tonight at dinner."

Rita held the door open for Tayler. "Honey, let's change yo' shoes before we go anywhere."

After Tayler changed into a pair of black sneakers, Rita walked her through the flower gardens and past the hammocks and chaise lounge chairs. Rita pointed out the entrance to a nature trail should Tayler find herself up for a scenic stroll.

"All of this is so impressive. You must love living here," Tayler said.

"Oh, I don't live here."

"I'm sorry, I thought you and Wallace were like the innkeepers."

Rita laughed and took a rubber band from her wrist and pulled her hair into a ponytail. "No, honey, Rollin is Wallace's nephew. We live over in Garrard County. It's just about thirty minutes away."

"So, you don't regularly work here?"

"I do. I've been the housekeeper for almost a year now. The farm employs ten people, and then there's

Corra when she comes around. But Rollin runs the B and B mostly by himself now."

"Really! He doesn't look like an innkeeper, or B and B operator, and he has all this land to take care of as well. That's amazing." Tayler turned around and glanced across the fields, where several people worked in the distance.

"Honey, you haven't seen anything yet. Come on, let's make our way back up to the house. I need to get dinner started and you should take a nap."

Tayler matched strides with Rita as they headed back to the house. "That's something I plan to do a lot of while I'm here. Napping and resting. And that garden back there looks like the perfect spot."

"Yes, it's very relaxing after a hard day's work."

Tayler sighed, thinking about lounging in the hammock with a tall glass of lemonade and her favorite self-help book. Nicole was right—this vacation would be good for her. She'd return home relaxed and ready to tackle the world again.

Around dinnertime, Tayler heard the other guests as they walked up and down the hall. She'd had a shower and a good nap and felt refreshed and alive. Some of the stress and tension from maneuvering Chicago's highways and trains on a daily basis had already started to leave her body. Dressed in a pale yellow and white sundress that she'd purchased at Bloomingdale's just for this trip, she went downstairs to join the others.

The couples at the table introduced themselves and entertained Tayler with tales from their family reunion. Rita served some of the best fried chicken Tayler had ever put in her mouth, and she couldn't stop complimenting her on everything. After dinner the other guests prepared to attend a dance, which one of the men didn't seem too eager about.

"I'm going because that's why we came down here. But I'm just saying, a Danville dance is nothing like going to a club in Atlanta."

"Forrest," his wife said, busting him out, "when was the last time you stepped inside a club, anyway? You go down to the Crows Nest for a drink once every six months, but I wouldn't call that clubbing. Don't lie to these people."

"Barbara, I'm not lying and you know it. Plus, I didn't say I went clubbing, I just said they don't compare. Folks around here do things at a much slower pace."

"Don't y'all listen to Forrest. This man is in bed by nine thirty every night. He hasn't seen the inside of a nightclub since we got married fifteen years ago. He'll be down there tonight dancing his butt off."

Everyone at the table laughed.

"Tayler, you're welcome to join us, if you want," Barbara said.

"Thank you, but I think I'm going to get some work done and hit the sack early."

"Smart woman," Forrest said. "We all need to be ready in the morning."

The kitchen door swung open and Rollin, dressed in jeans and a casual button-down shirt, walked into the room.

"Rollin, we were just about to ask Rita where you were."

"Good evening, everybody. How was your dinner?" he asked as Rita began to clear the table.

Forrest reared back in his seat. "That was the best meal I believe I've ever had. I'm gonna have to loosen my belt up before my stomach explodes."

Everyone at the table chuckled.

"Mrs. Rita, my compliments to the chef," Forrest continued.

"Well, thank you."

"Tomorrow morning I'll be thankful for this meal," Forrest said in a loud playful voice, and everyone at the table broke out into laughter again.

There was an inside joke there, Tayler knew, but she hadn't been let in on it. She had that odd-man-out feeling again and wanted to return to her room and her laptop.

"Tayler, how long will you be staying?" Barbara asked.

"For a month, possibly two."

Eyebrows rose and surprised looks came from around the table. "That's a nice long time. Rita might put you to work in the kitchen," Forrest said with a chuckle.

Rita laughed while she and Rollin picked up the glasses from the table.

"Rollin, who you got coming in after we check out?" Forrest asked.

"Nobody right now. We'll have a few vacancies."

Tayler didn't know if it was her imagination or not, but everyone at the table seemed to turn and stare at her with smiles on their faces. It took a few minutes before Rollin's statement registered. After they left, she would be the only guest, alone with Rollin.

"Anybody ready for some hot apple pie with ice cream?" Rita asked.

Every hand at the table went up except Tayler's. Suddenly, she had a sick feeling in the pit of her stomach.

"Nicole, you didn't tell me I would be here with him alone. The guests are checking out in a few days and nobody else is checking in. Girl, I can't stay here with this man by myself." Tayler paced the floor of her bedroom holding her cell phone to her ear.

"Tayler, what are you worried about? It's a B and B—somebody is always checking in and out. Besides, you know I wouldn't have suggested you go down there if Rollin wasn't cool. He's a businessman, for Christ's sake. What do you think the man's gonna do, jump your bones once everyone leaves? And that house is the bomb, isn't it?"

"Yes, it's beautiful, but what if nobody checks in? I'd feel more comfortable in a hotel."

"What? Are you crazy? That's the perfect place to relax and get your head together. No stress, no pressure. Just smell the roses, if you know what I mean. And Rollin is as fine a gentleman as you'll ever meet."

"I don't know about that," Tayler said, almost under her breath. He was fine as hell, but she hadn't met that gentleman yet.

"Girl, unpack your bags and chill. You deserve to enjoy yourself. Sit on the front porch and read a book or something. Does Rita still make pitchers of lemonade every afternoon?"

"Yes, she does." That was one of the personal touches Tayler liked about the house. When they came in from the tour earlier, Rita had placed two pitchers in the library. One was full of lemonade, and another full of water with orange slices.

Tayler let out a loud sigh as she pulled back the comforter and sat down. "I suppose somebody else could check in. I guess it won't be so bad."

"Of course not," Nicole said. "Now tell me what you think of Rollin. He's single, you know."

Tayler knew to keep her thoughts about Rollin to herself. Nicole couldn't keep her mouth shut about anything. Tayler wanted to say, "He's fine as a glass of Bordeaux but rude as hell," but instead she said, "He seems like a nice man."

"He is, and I just know you two will hit it off."

"Nicole, I came here to rest, not get hooked up with your cousin—you do know that, don't you?"

"Ah, girl, yeah, I'm just messing with you. Besides, what would you do with a farmer?"

Tayler thought of a few things she could *do* with one farmer in particular.

Chapter 3

*K*nock, knock.

Tayler pulled the covers over her head. She had to be dreaming about a crazy person knocking on the door.

Knock, knock.

What the hell? She rolled over from one side to the other. Was she dreaming or was the place suddenly under construction?

"Tayler, it's time for breakfast." *Knock, knock.* "Are you up?"

Was somebody calling her name? Was that Rollin? She threw the covers back and pushed her eye mask up into her bonnet.

"Tayler, breakfast in fifteen minutes—come on down. The truck leaves at seven a.m., and you don't want to miss it."

What the hell!

Tayler sat up and reached for her robe. She wasn't hungry, and she wasn't going to breakfast.

She wrapped herself in her robe and went to open the door. She cracked the door and glanced up into Rollin's scowling face.

"Good morning. I see you're not up yet. Well, you might want to grab a shower and come on down. Breakfast will be served in the dining room and we're heading out at seven o'clock on the nose."

"I'm sorry, but heading out where?"

"The vegetable garden first, then we'll swing by—"

"Hold up. I'll skip the garden tour this morning, if you don't mind. I'm on vacation. What time is it, anyway?" She looked behind her and didn't see one peek of light coming through the blinds. It was still dark out.

"It's five thirty a.m., and unless you don't plan to eat today, you need to be on the truck before seven a.m."

"What truck?"

"Didn't Nicole tell you that this is a working farm? We go out each morning to pick food for lunch and dinner."

"Wait a minute." She shook her head. "This is what kind of a farm?"

Rollin shook his head. "Get dressed and come on down. I'll explain it to you. Looks like Nicole forgot to tell you a few things."

He walked down the hall and left Tayler standing in the doorway watching his back. Once he disappeared down the steps, she closed the door and threw herself against it.

What the hell have I gotten myself into?

She staggered into the shower then made it downstairs well before seven. Everyone was still at the table eating when she walked into the room.

"Grab a plate, honey. You've got fifteen minutes before the truck leaves," Rita informed Tayler.

The smell of bacon, pancakes and hot biscuits left Tayler speechless and looking around the room for a plate. She wasn't hungry and had intended to negotiate her way back into bed.

"Here's a plate."

Tayler turned at the sound of Rollin's voice. He stood next to the buffet offering her a square blue-and-white plate.

"I suggest you eat something. Going out on the truck to pick your own food is part of the charm of staying on a working farm."

He glanced down at Tayler's sneaker-clad feet. "Once you get out there, just follow Kevin's instructions and you'll be fine."

After accepting the plate, Tayler glanced at her watch. "So, I now have about ten minutes to eat something and grab a cup of coffee."

"Hot coffee's down there." Rollin pointed to the end of the server table.

Tayler set her plate down and opted for a hot cup of coffee instead. A white carafe and a couple of cups sat around waiting for someone to try them. She poured herself a cup of what looked like liquid mud. Desperate for caffeine, she decided against her better judgment, and took a sip.

She almost dropped her cup, "What the hell is this?"

Rollin walked over to her. "It's called coffee. It's organic. A dark roast decaf. I whip it up for guests daily."

She sat her cup down on the server and pressed her

fingers against her lips. "Thank you but I'll pass on the...coffee."

Every morning she stopped at Starbucks for a cup of blond-roast coffee. How was she supposed to function without her coffee?

"Herbal tea is better for you anyway," Rollin said. "If you haven't tried it before Rita will show you our impressive collection."

Tayler cleared her throat. *This fool expects me to go out and pick food at seven o'clock in the morning without a cup of coffee. He must be off his rocker.* "Do you know anywhere I can get a *good* cup of coffee?"

Rollin shook his head and laughed. "Try a cup of tea, or some orange juice. You've only got a little more than five minutes now." He walked away.

There was no way she could wolf down breakfast in five minutes, so she grabbed a piece of toast and poured herself a glass of orange juice. Before she could finish, everyone was ready to go.

As much as she wanted to protest and drive into town for a cup of coffee, she conformed and walked out to the truck with everyone else. She was going to kick Nicole's ass for this one.

"First time?"

Tayler whipped her head around and looked into the blue eyes of a young boy who looked as if he was still in high school. His white skin, kissed by the sun, was almost as bronzed as hers.

He held out his hand. "I'm Kevin. Need some help up?"

"You're seriously taking us out on this rusted-out truck with no seats in the back?"

"Yep, unless you'd rather walk. It's about five miles back up the road."

She held out her hand. "Kevin, I'm Tayler, and I have a feeling we'll be seeing a lot of each other."

He grasped her hand and elbow to help her up onto the truck. "I'll be lookin' forward to it."

The ride out was bumpy and rough. Tayler couldn't even enjoy the view, her butt hurt so badly. She held on for dear life and tried to avoid getting her new sneakers dirty.

Kevin led them through the fields and Tayler picked whatever she saw everybody else picking. She wasn't into this getting-back-to-nature stuff. The only thing she wanted to get back to was the house so she could get on her cell and cuss Nicole out.

"Barbara, think you've got enough green beans? Why not move on down and get some cucumbers. I like them in my salad."

"Forrest, get your own cucumbers. We're trying to show Tayler here how to pick beans. I may not have lived in the county for a while now, but I'm still a country girl."

Tayler compared the small amount of beans in her basket to the overflowing amount in Barbara's. She had to admit she needed the help.

"Honey, the truck's not gonna be out here all day, so you need to pick faster. Here, let me show you how. Sit that basket down. You need both hands."

Tayler did as she was told, and in no time at all, her basket was overflowing as well.

"Thank you. This is the first time I've ever picked anything."

"Fun, isn't it?"

Tayler glanced down at her dusty sneakers and dirty manicured nails. *Hell, no, this isn't fun.* "I guess, yeah."

Barbara laughed. "Don't worry, you'll get the hang of it. Before you leave you'll be a pro at picking beans and anything else you want to eat. Once we leave, I guess Rita or Kevin will ride out with you every day."

Tayler stopped in her tracks. "You have to do this every day?"

"Sure, that's what staying on an organic farm is all about. Everything's fresh right from the garden. Wait until dinner tonight—you'll see what I mean then."

Barbara picked up her basket and started walking away.

"What if I'm not able to make it out here every morning?" Tayler asked. "Surely Rita will prepare something anyway."

"Maybe, but why wouldn't you want to?" Barbara stopped and turned to face Tayler. "That's what people stay here for, the holistic experience. Isn't that why you're here?"

Holistic, as in back to nature, organic, oh, hell! Tayler gave a slow nod of her head. "Sure, it's just some mornings I might be working, and I wondered how they'd handle that, you know. Let's say I miss the truck or something."

"Don't worry, I'm sure Rollin won't let you starve," Barbara responded with a laugh.

"He just might," Tayler mumbled, remembering how rude he'd been to her.

"Honey, as pretty as you are, I wouldn't be surprised if Rollin doesn't offer to pick your food for you. I don't know him that well, but I saw the way he looked at you this morning."

"What do you mean? How did he look at me?" Tayler asked, apprehensive about the answer.

"Let's just say I noticed him noticing you. That's all. Come on, let's go pick some blackberries—Rita promised me a cobbler after dinner."

After a brief stop back at the truck for a bottle of water and a new basket, Tayler tried to talk Barbara into letting her wait by the truck, but she wouldn't hear of it.

"If you're going to be out here after we leave, you need to learn a thing or two," she insisted. "Come on, city girl."

With the sleeve of her shirt, Tayler wiped the sweat from her brow and followed Barbara along a path that lead to blackberry bushes. Hot, tired and ready for a bath, Tayler could barely muster up the energy to pick berries.

"Okay, honey, dig in. But be careful, they have thorns. And remember, the blacker the berry, the sweeter the juice," she said with a laugh. "Oh, I love that saying."

Tayler chuckled and shook her head.

"No, seriously, though, the blacker and plumper the berry, the better. The red or purple ones aren't ripe yet, so leave them. And don't be afraid to get under there and find them berries. They're tough—you can't hurt anything."

But my hands, Tayler thought. Then, she realized the sooner they had enough berries, the sooner they would be out of there, so she held back the thorns with one hand and plucked off berries with the other.

A few minutes later, she moved down farther in search of more plump blackberries. She was starting to get the hang of it and had only been pricked by thorns twice. She crouched down when she saw a bunch of blackberries close to the ground. Careful this time, she pulled the thorns back with one hand and reached in with the other.

Suddenly, a long black snake slithered from the open path, headed in her direction.

"Ahh!" She screamed, jumped to her feet and ran as if her life depended upon it.

Before she could catch her breath, she ran into a brick wall named Rollin.

"Hey, what's going on?" he asked as he reached out and caught Tayler by the arm.

"A snake!" She flung her arms and looked back over her shoulder. "A snake attacked me back there. It crawled out from under the bushes and came right at me." She shook her hands before brushing down her pant legs.

"Did it bite you?" he asked.

All she could do was shake her head.

"How big was it?" he asked, holding her now with one arm around her shoulders to steady her.

She took a deep breath. "I don't know, it wasn't too big, but it was a snake nonetheless. Yuck, I hate snakes." She swatted at the crawling sensation going up her arm.

"What color was it?"

Now everything on her body itched, and Tayler pulled away long enough to shake her pant legs and notice the smirk on Rollin's face. "I think it was black, or…what's so funny? Are you laughing at me?"

"No, of course not," he said as he pointed behind her. "Is that it?"

Without looking behind her, Tayler jumped and ran behind Rollin, and then glanced at the ground. She didn't see anything.

The roar of laughter caught her attention and she looked up at everyone in the truck bed having a good laugh at her expense.

Rollin chuckled and held his hands up, palms out. "I'm sorry, that was mean. I shouldn't have done it."

Barbara called out, trying not to laugh, "Tayler, we're sorry, but it was only a small garden snake. It won't hurt you."

With her arms crossed, Tayler glared at Barbara and the crew. "It was a snake, that's all I know, and I don't do snakes."

"Occasionally, a little snake crawls under the bushes looking for a nice warm bed. Come show me where you saw it." Rollin touched Tayler's elbow, edging her back down the path.

Arms crossed, she stood rooted to her spot. "I'm not going back down there. I told you, I don't do snakes."

Kevin walked up. "Is she okay?" he asked Rollin.

"Yeah, she'll be fine."

"It was probably a garden snake, like Mrs. Barbara said," Kevin offered. "They're virtually harmless, and they do their best to avoid people. I don't see too many of them out here."

Kevin and Rollin walked down the path in the direction of the snake. They poked around under bushes, but it didn't look as if either spotted the snake. Rollin picked up her basket of blackberries. She wondered what she was going to eat every day, since she wasn't about to come back out here to pick anything.

Back at the truck, Tayler sat on the edge of the bed, trying to get her hands to stop shaking. A snake! A damned snake! If anyone had told her they had snakes here, she would have stayed in Chicago.

Rollin and Kevin made their way back to the truck, laughing with each other. No doubt she was the topic of conversation.

"Glad I could make your day, fellas," she said.

Rollin looked from Kevin back to her. "I'm sorry, we weren't talking about you. Here's your blackberries." He set the basket next to her.

"Thank you."

"I'm sorry your first morning turned out to be such a dramatic one. Guests usually don't encounter snakes this soon."

"So it usually takes a few days before snakes show up?" she asked sarcastically.

"Oh, they're out here every day. You startled that one, that's all. Next time, make some noise and it'll slither away."

"Next time! Oh, I don't plan on coming back out here. I'll eat all my meals in town if I have to."

Rollin nodded. "That'll get pretty expensive."

"I can afford it."

"Maybe you can." He stretched his arms over his head. "Guess I was right when I said you might not last a month. I can spot a quitter from miles away."

He touched a nerve and she straightened up. "I'm not a quitter. I just don't play with snakes."

He shrugged. "Just stay out of the blackberry

bushes, then everything will be okay. What do you say?"

She looked at his outstretched hand, waiting for her to accept it, then looked away. She wasn't making any promises.

"What do you have to lose? You'll eat some good food and might even make a new friend."

She raised a brow at him. "*You* want to be my new friend?"

"I wasn't thinking about me, but Rita. She'll be disappointed if she can't cook for you. After these guys leave she won't have guest to cook for."

He still hadn't persuaded her.

"Say yes, and I'll do my best to keep the snakes away."

He smiled and those big dimples mesmerized her. It took a few seconds to turn from his gaze and pull herself together.

"Okay, but no more blackberries." She accepted his hand.

Chapter 4

The next morning, no one rode to the fields because, luckily, they'd picked enough food the day before.

Tayler took advantage of the free time and ventured out to the porch after breakfast with her laptop. Minutes later, Forrest joined her.

"This feels wonderful, doesn't it?"

Tayler turned to Forrest, who sat in one of the big white rocking chairs across the porch from her.

"Yes, it does. We have a nice breeze." She smiled and turned back to her laptop.

"You don't get this in the city." He took a deep breath. "Just smell that air. No car exhaust or garbage. Just clean country air, the way God intended it to be."

Tayler cut her eyes at Forrest. *What's so damned special about the air?*

"What's that you're working on? I thought you said you were on vacation."

"I am, but I'm still trying to keep up with work—you know how it is. It's hard to take a vacation when you have so many responsibilities."

He crossed his legs in her direction. "So what do you do?"

She took a deep breath and thought of a way to explain what she did so he'd understand. "I oversee a team that installs data communications lines all around the world."

Forrest whistled. "Sounds like a lot of work. Too bad they can't manage without you."

"Oh, they can. I just like to keep tabs on everything."

"So you're somewhat of a micromanager?"

"No, not really." She hated that phrase. "I just like to be available if I'm needed."

"We used to have backups for vacations and such."

"I have a backup."

"Incompetent, though, huh?"

"He doesn't handle things the way I do, but he's very competent."

Forrest laughed.

She smiled but didn't get the joke. "What's so funny?"

The front door opened as Forrest stood up and pointed at her laptop. "You need to look up 'micromanager,'" he said as he walked over to hold the door for his wife.

Tayler crossed her arms and gave him a knowing smile. She understood.

Barbara walked over to Tayler. "Well, Tayler, it was nice meeting you, but we're gonna have to get on the road." Tayler moved her laptop aside and stood up to hug the older woman goodbye. Within minutes, everyone else came out to say goodbye. Rita and Tayler stood on the porch waving as both cars pulled off. The moment reminded Tayler of a scene from an old movie.

"Well, young lady, what have you got planned for today?" Rita asked.

Tayler sat back down and picked up her laptop. "I was going to get some work done, but I've changed my mind. I think I'll just enjoy the breeze."

"That sounds nice. You enjoy yourself, now. I'm gonna go up and start cleaning those rooms. Lunch is at noon."

"Okay, I'll see you then."

Tayler thought about what Forrest had said and closed her laptop. She wasn't a micromanager.

A few minutes later, she heard a vehicle barreling up the driveway. A big black truck that resembled a monster with tinted windows pulled in next to her BMW. She'd seen the truck parked around back before but wasn't sure who it belonged to. It kicked dust all over her precious jewel.

The door opened, and Rollin stepped out. Tayler rolled her eyes and mumbled under her breath, "I should have known."

He walked up onto the porch. "Enjoying yourself?" he asked.

"Yes, I'm just relaxing." She followed his gaze to her laptop. "And trying to stay away from work."

"Yeah, Nicole said you were here to get away from work. She said you needed to get some rest," he said.

She glanced over her shoulder as he now stood at the door. "And I plan to get plenty of that, as long as

I don't have to adhere to six a.m. wake-up calls every morning."

"You must plan on losing at lot of weight, then."

She set her laptop aside and turned around in her seat. "So, let's talk about that. Do you really expect me to go out there all by myself and pick vegetables every morning?"

He left the entrance front door and walked over to stand against the railing opposite of her. "Sure, I do. This is a *working* organic farm. People come from all over for the opportunity to pick their own food and have Rita prepare it for them. Almost everything we make here is fresh and from scratch. Tomorrow, I'll take you out and introduce you to the hens."

Tayler laughed. "You talk about hens like they're people."

His lips pressed together in a slight grimace. "No, but I think a proper introduction should be made before you stick your hand under her ass to pick up the eggs."

Eyes wide, Tayler pointed to herself. "Oh, *no*, my hands won't be going under anything's ass. Besides, I don't have to eat eggs. Pancakes are fine with me."

He chuckled. "You need an egg for pancakes."

"Then I'll have a bagel."

He shook his head. "No bagels, nor doughnuts, before you ask."

She brought her palm to her forehead and massaged it for a moment. "Seriously, though, how do I get a good meal without playing farmer Jane? And what about the elderly? Surely to God, you don't make them ride out on that old rusted truck."

"They appreciate it the most. But if you want to

eat somewhere else, there's always Donita's Diner in town."

"And how do I get there?"

"Take the main road back into town and you'll see it on your right. The green-and-white sign kind of jumps out at you."

"Thank you. I think I'll try it."

He walked back to the front door. "Suit yourself, but I think you'll be disappointed."

"As long as I don't have to pick the food myself, I'll enjoy it."

Rollin went inside and Tayler opened her computer back up. She hadn't been able to catch Nicole by phone, so she sent her another email. She was going to wring that chick's neck.

A few minutes later, Rita poked her head out the door and announced that lemonade would be served in the library.

"Rita, you didn't have to go to any trouble for me."

"Honey, it's no trouble at all. Besides, around here folks is dropping by all the time. Come on in and help yourself."

Tayler went inside for her afternoon treat. First, she ran upstairs and grabbed her book. The minute she opened the door to head back outside with her goods, two children came barreling through the door, screaming as they shot past her.

She spun around and almost dropped her glass.

"I smell cookies, I smell cookies," they screamed.

Kids. Please don't tell me they've come to stay. She could hear her peace coming to an end.

Juggling her lemonade, cookies and book, she continued out onto the porch to retain her seat.

"You must be Tayler," a woman who didn't look a day over twenty asked as she came up the steps.

"How did I give myself away?"

"Rollin said you were the only guest."

"Oh, that made it easy."

"Hi, I'm Corra, his sister." She held out her hand.

Tayler juggled a hand free. "Hold on, let me set some of this down." She placed everything on the table next to her laptop and shook the woman's hand. "It's nice to meet you, Corra. Do the little ones belong to you?"

"Yes, those are mine. They smelled Rita's chocolate chip cookies the minute they stepped out of the car. I swear, it's like they're cookie bloodhounds."

Tayler chuckled. "They are good."

Corra placed a hand on her large hips. "I need cookies like I need a hole in my head, so I'll take your word for it."

Tayler returned to her seat.

"Are you enjoying your stay so far?"

"Yes, I am. This is a lovely place."

Corra walked over and sat in the swing across from Tayler's rocking chair. "I hope Rollin is being hospitable."

"He is, and so is Rita. Everyone's been very nice."

"Well, that's good. Rollin said you're staying for a month, is that right?"

Tayler sipped her lemonade and nodded. "Yes, maybe longer. I'm not sure yet."

"Wow, where do you work that you can take that much time off? I've been at Save-A-Lot for over three years and all I get is a lousy two weeks."

"I work for MesaCom, a small telecommunications

company. I needed to get out of the city, so I took some extra vacation time."

"Oh, I see. Is that your laptop?" she asked, noticing it on the table next to Tayler.

"Yeah."

"Are you pretty good with computers?"

"I think so."

"Great. We're having a fund-raiser for Roosevelt Elementary trying to put a computer in every classroom. You'd think the board would supply something so vital nowadays, but no, they're too busy making sure their members get raises."

"That's definitely a worthy cause. Every child today should have a computer. If not, they'll get left behind."

"Girl, that's what I've been saying. But you know trying to convince some of them board members of that is like trying to talk a turtle into running a marathon. The PTA's taken it upon ourselves to raise the money. Maybe you can help since you're going to be here for a month or longer?"

With raised brows, Tayler gave it some thought. "Uh, sure. Let me know what I can do."

"Great." Corra jumped up as her children came barreling back out the front door and dashed out into the yard.

"Jamie, Katie, where are you going?" she yelled after them.

"Looking for Uncle Rollin," one of them called back as they rounded the house.

Corra turned back to Tayler. "Do you have any children?"

"No, I don't."

"Think long and hard before you do. They'll test your nerves."

Then Corra got up and disappeared inside the house.

Smiling, Tayler put her feet up and opened her book.

The next morning, bright and early, Tayler heard a light tapping on her bedroom door. "Oh, no," she whispered and pulled the covers over her head.

"Tayler, honey. I fixed you some breakfast before you go out with Kevin this morning," Rita said.

Tayler threw the covers back and grabbed her robe. *Will these people ever let me sleep in?* She flung the robe around her body and tied the sash before throwing the door open.

"Thank you, Rita, but I'm going to skip breakfast and the ride with Kevin this morning. I'll eat in town later."

Rita looked taken aback.

"I'm sorry. I told Rollin I wouldn't be going picking, or whatever, this morning. He should have told you."

"Yes, he should have. Well, if you change your mind, I'll wrap a plate up for you and put it in the refrigerator."

Three hours later, Tayler walked out of her room dressed in a pair of jeans, a new signature T-shirt and her favorite three-inch strappy sandals. Now she was ready for breakfast. She'd be damned if she was going to spend her vacation jumping up every morning to go pick something.

The house was quiet again, which was a little eerie to her. She descended the grand staircase with purse in hand and felt like a queen or princess or something. The railing was magnificently designed. She looked around downstairs and found a radio playing in the library, but no occupant.

She walked out to her car and noticed a tractor in the distance and wondered if that was Rollin hard at work. She opened the car door and tossed her purse inside. It was time to ride into Danville and see what was up.

Tayler had no idea where she was going, but she remembered Rollin telling her a diner was just inside town. She rolled her window down and then scanned radio stations trying to find something other than country music. She finally located a hip-hop station. Glancing at the clock, she figured Nicole should be at her desk by now and pulled out her cell phone.

"Good morning, Nicole Burns."

"I figured I'd catch your ass at work, since you seem to be dodging my calls."

"Tayler! Hey, girl, how's it going?"

"Didn't you get any of my voice messages or emails?"

Nicole laughed. "Girl, that riding-out-on-the-truck thing must be something new. I didn't know about that."

"So, not only am I the only guest here, but Rollin expects me to ride out every morning with this young guy I don't know to pick my own damn food. Not to mention their coffee is the worst I've ever had. I'm going into town for a cup now."

"Come on, Tayler, relax and get into it. Life in the country is different than life in Chicago."

"I know that. But I booked myself into a B and B

hoping to get a little rest. So far, I've been awakened before the break of dawn and forced to work without coffee. I rode in the bed of a dirty rusted-out truck. Oh, and a snake chased me through the fields. Does that sound like I'm relaxing to you?"

Nothing but laughter came from the other end of the phone, which pissed Tayler off.

"I'm glad you find this so freakin' amusing."

"I don't mean to laugh at you, but you should hear yourself. You've been there two days and you sound like a spoiled brat. You're in the country, Tayler. There are snakes and old trucks in the country. You're out of your element, but that's what you needed. You'll survive without Starbucks for a little while."

"What are you now, my therapist?"

"No, but I know what you need. I hope you haven't been on that computer, either. Read a book, go for long walks and see if Rita will let you help her in the garden. Get back to nature for a minute."

Now Tayler had to laugh. "You set me up, didn't you? You knew all along this wasn't going to be what I expected."

"No, that's not true."

Tayler took a deep breath as she approached town. "Nicole, you owe me for this, that's all I'm saying. If I even end up staying the month, you owe me dinner at Spiaggia's when I get back."

"Girl, you got it. Just try to relax and destress. I hate to cut you off, but I've gotta run to a meeting. Stay in touch."

"Oh, I most certainly will." Tayler hung up just as she saw a large tattered green-and-white sign come into view. Donita's Diner. The sign was set close to the road, most likely so guests didn't drive by too fast and miss the diner. She pulled into the lot and killed the engine. The outside had seen better days and could use a paint job. She hoped the inside would fare better.

The minute she opened the door, she knew she was in trouble. The heavy smells of grease and cigarette smoke hung in the air. A tired-looking middle-aged waitress greeted Tayler and led her across the sticky floor to a table. Tayler tried not to slip and fall. After the waitress recited the morning special, Tayler ordered a cup of coffee and a three-egg omelet.

"Is this seat taken?"

She looked up from the menu she'd kept to see Officer Greg holding the chair across from her, dressed in his snug-fitting uniform.

Chapter 5

Tayler gestured to the empty chair across from her in answer to Greg's question. "No, help yourself." However, a quick sweep of the room revealed plenty of empty chairs.

"You're the young lady staying out at Coleman House, right?"

"Yes, you stopped me and escorted me in the other day. You're Greg, right?"

"Greg Mason." He extended his hand.

She accepted it. "Tayler Carter." She had peeped Office Greg's rugged good looks when he had pulled her over. Now, she noticed his muscular physique, as well.

"It's nice to meet you, Tayler. I thought I recognized you. Is this your first time in Danville?"

"Yes, it is. I'm on vacation."

"Where you from?"

"Chicago."

"So, how do you like our little town?"

"I haven't seen much outside of the ride into town, and then to here this morning."

"Then you'll have to let me give you the ten-cent tour."

The waitress returned with two cups of coffee and their food. Tayler assumed Officer Greg was a regular, since the waitress knew what he wanted to eat.

"I'm surprised you're not eating at Coleman House. Rita's one of the best cooks in the county."

Tayler blew on her piping-hot coffee. "So I've heard, but I'm not too keen on having to pick my own food every day."

He nodded in agreement as he began eating.

Tayler sliced into her omelet as melted cheese oozed all over the plate. Then she bit into crunchy vegetables. She chewed them up enough to swallow, then chased it down with a little coffee that activated her gag reflex.

Greg laughed. "Yeah, the coffee's an acquired taste."

She wrinkled her nose and pushed the cup away. "That's coffee?"

He laughed harder, and then leaned into the table. "Stop out at the Speedway gas station and you can get a better cup. But don't tell anybody I told you that."

"Thanks," she whispered, and gave him a coconspirator nod.

She played with the rest of her food while Greg finished his so fast she was sure he'd have indigestion later.

After breakfast he walked her out to her car. "I was

serious about that tour. If you're not busy when I get off, I can come out and pick you up."

He's persistent—how sweet.

"Maybe another time. I'm still trying to rest up from the drive down."

"Well, if you change your mind—" he produced a business card "—give me a call."

She took the card and glanced at it before shoving it into her purse. "Sure."

Tayler found the Speedway gas station on her way back to the house and purchased a large cup of coffee. Greg was right—this was coffee.

When she pulled up to the house, Rita and Rollin stood on the front porch. She hesitated with her coffee cup in hand but decided to go ahead since this wouldn't be the only morning she went out for coffee.

As she walked up the steps, Rollin gazed down at her in a way that made the hair on the back of her neck stand up.

"I see you found some coffee."

She held up the cup. "It's not Starbucks, but there's nothing like a shot of caffeine to get the juices flowing."

"Then you're probably ready to do some running around. Why don't you change shoes and ride over to Houchen's with me?"

"Are you going to put me to work once we get there?"

He smiled. "Probably so."

"Rollin, just make sure you get her back here for lunch," Rita said. "I'm gonna start picking those beans Kevin brought in earlier." Rita disappeared into the house.

"Exactly what is Houchen's?" Tayler asked.

"A hardware store. I ordered a new tiller."

"And I have to change shoes for that?"

He glanced down at her sandals. "Not really. Come on."

She followed him out to his monster truck. He had on jeans, his work boots and another black T-shirt. She'd bet he had no idea how that casual laid-back style made him look so sexy. He opened the door for her and tried to help her up, but she started falling backward. Before she could fall on her butt, Rollin caught her in his arms. He looked at the covered coffee cup in her hand, and let out a sigh of relief.

"Sorry about this," Rollin said before placing his hand on her butt and heaving her up into the truck.

Tayler's eyes widened as she went sailing up into the seat. He closed her door, and she tried not to think about his hand on her butt as she placed her coffee in the cup holder.

Rollin jumped in and started the engine. After he pulled out onto the main road, he turned on the radio.

"How did you like your breakfast?" he asked.

"I didn't. But somehow I believe you already knew that."

"I never said it was good. I just said it was a place to get breakfast."

"A breakfast biscuit from anywhere would have tasted better."

"No, you would have been better off with Rita's breakfast."

"You're right. Officer Greg says she's the best cook in the county."

"You ran into him at the diner?"

"He ran into me, actually."

"Yeah, he eats most of his meals there."

"He offered me a tour of the town this afternoon."

Rollin turned and looked at her for a second before shaking his head. "Greg doesn't waste any time."

"That's what I thought."

"You turned him down?"

"I said maybe another time. He's a cop. I don't want to make him mad—he might find a way to write me a ticket for the other day."

Rollin threw his head back and laughed. "Greg wouldn't do that even if he could. He's a pretty decent guy."

They rode on in silence for a few minutes before Rollin spoiled the moment.

"So, Nicole said you had a breakdown or something at work. And this vacation is supposed to destress you, is that right?"

Tayler's head swiveled so fast she heard her neck crack. *What the hell.* "When did she tell you that?" Tayler knew Nicole couldn't keep anything to herself.

"When she said you wanted to stay for a month. I asked why so long."

Tayler shook her head in disbelief. "It wasn't a breakdown. I snapped on somebody that I shouldn't have, that's all. And since I never take time off, this vacation is long overdue."

"I hope you don't mind that she told me. I told her I was thinking about closing down."

Tayler's eyes widened as a hand flew to her chest. "Don't tell me you're staying open because of me."

He laughed as he pulled the truck into Houchen's parking lot. "Of course not. Whatever business decision I make won't take place right away." He turned off the engine and opened the door to the truck. "Come on in. I might need you to help me carry the tiller."

She glared at him and then waited for him to come around and help her out. As she followed him around the hardware store, she wondered what else Nicole had told him. What did he know about her that she wasn't aware of?

After Rollin picked up the tiller and had it loaded onto the bed of his truck, they headed back to the farm.

"I don't know the first thing about farming, but that tiller looks too small for all the large fields around here," she said.

"Good observation. It's for the gardens out back. We use large cultivators for the fields."

"Oh. Well, like I said, I don't know much about farms or gardens."

"That's okay." He glanced over at her hands. "You might get your hands dirty, but I'll teach you something before you leave here. After all, this is a working farm."

"Wow, I'm really looking forward to that." She tried to scale back the sarcasm in her statement.

He laughed. "We'll get back in time for lunch, but I need to drop this tiller off first. You don't mind, do you?"

"No. It's not like I have anything else to do."

He turned onto another road that led to a large old barn.

"This is a back entrance to the farm," he said.

Tayler was amazed at how much land the farm consisted of. Rollin backed his truck up to a big red barn. The doors slid open and Kevin walked out.

"Is that Ms. Carter?" Kevin asked as he walked up to the passenger side of the truck.

She stuck her head out the window. "Please, call me Tayler." What was she, an old lady or something?

"She rode into town with me. Come on, Kev, help me get this thing out."

"Missed you this morning," Kevin said as he tapped her on the hand before turning back to the truck bed.

"She had breakfast at Donita's," Rollin said with a smile.

Kevin looked back at Tayler. "Oh, no," he laughed into his balled fist. "Bet you won't do that again."

"Somebody should have warned me," she said, as she opened the door and climbed out of the truck herself this time.

"I said you'd be disappointed," Rollin added.

When Rollin and Kevin lifted the tiller off the back of the truck, Tayler couldn't help but notice the muscles in Rollin's arms. But she turned away before he caught her staring.

"Come on in, have a look around," Rollin said, as Kevin walked ahead of him, pulling the tiller.

Tayler followed him inside, carefully watching her every step. Aside from the dirty floor, the inside of the barn was surprisingly neat. Everything was stacked up and organized. She'd expected to see some farm animals, but only neatly organized tools lined the walls.

Rollin looked back at her. "What's wrong? Scared you'll get your new sandals dirty?"

Kevin laughed as he pulled the tiller farther back into another part of the barn and disappeared.

"They're not new." She brought her hand to her nose. "Is that manure I smell?"

"No, that's compost, and a bunch of other stuff. The only manure we use is green manure mix."

Rollin led her to an area of the barn where long pieces of wood and boxes sat. "This here's my new greenhouse. It's in pieces now, but I should have it up in a couple of days."

She stood next to him, noticing how proud he was of his new greenhouse. "What grows in there?" she asked.

"I'm starting a crop of greens, which are in high demand. Collard greens, turnip greens and some spinach. I'm not sure what else."

"You're really into digging in the dirt, aren't you?"

He laughed. "I own a farm—that's what I do. Why are you so opposed to it?"

She crossed her arms. "I'm not. If that's your thing, that's cool. Somebody has to do it, right?"

He crossed his arms. "Right. You know, you remind me of this prissy girl I went to school with."

Her jaw dropped. "Excuse me!"

"I don't mean it in a bad way. I'm just saying you're like a black Barbie doll." He smiled as if he'd just complimented her.

"No, farmer Rollin, I'm not a Barbie. I'm a city girl, born and raised. I don't dig or crawl around in the dirt or go pickin' vegetables in eighty-degree weather." She turned and headed for the barn door. "I'm out of here." She mumbled to herself, "A Barbie doll!"

Before she could reach the barn door, Rollin caught up with her. "Hold up. I didn't mean to insult you."

She stopped and turned around.

"I put my foot in my mouth. I'm sorry. Will you accept my apology?"

"Will you drive me back to the house?"

He drew in a deep breath and released it. "Yeah, come on. I'm ready to go."

Tayler marched out of the barn, eager to get back to the house and away from this rude, obnoxious, good-looking man. So walked with her head up and didn't see the pile of wet compost until she stepped into it.

"Oh, my God!" she screamed and hopped around on one foot.

Rollin laughed as he caught up with her and supported her by the arm. "Are you okay?"

"No, I just stepped in something brown and stinky. It touched my toes. I've got to get this shoe off!" she yelled. She tried to take the shoe off while hopping around on one foot.

Still laughing, Rollin swept her up in his arms. "It's compost—nothing more than plant and food waste. You'll be okay."

Tayler wrapped an arm around his neck to keep from falling. "What are you doing?"

He reached the truck and turned her so he could open the passenger side door. "I'm gonna take care of that for you. Sit right here."

She slid her arm from his neck and held her feet out while he opened the back door and returned with a towel.

"I bet you can't get that mess off my shoe. It's ruined."

He stepped one foot up on the footboard and laid the towel across his leg. He reached for her ankle and brought her foot to rest on his thigh. Tayler watched him maneuver the strap around her ankle until he released her foot from the shoe.

"You should have changed shoes like I suggested."

"We were just going to the hardware store, remember?" She looked down at the brown stains on her expensive designer shoe and sighed.

Rollin wiped the shoe off and set it down before wrapping the towel around her toes.

He held her foot in the palm of his hand. A shiver ran through her body as he wiped her toes one at a time. It felt good, but a little too sensual at the same time. She bit her lip and pulled back when it tickled.

He looked up at her. "I think I got it all."

She took a deep breath. "Thank you."

He slowly let go of her foot and shook the towel out.

Tayler scooted back in the seat and turned around so he could close the door. Her heart raced a mile a minute.

Rollin jumped back in the driver's seat and started the engine. He pulled off and glanced at Tayler.

"You know, you're welcome to spend all your time sitting on the porch or up in your room. But part of the objective of staying on an organic farm is learning about the food you eat. You're staying a month, so let me teach you a little something about organic food while you're here."

A month? We'll see. She tilted her head to the side. "Hmmm."

"I know you're used to being in charge at work, but you're on vacation. Embrace some new experiences. Become a student for a little while."

"If I become your pupil, do I still have to ride on the back of that truck every morning to *fetch* my food?"

"Yes, but you can sit up front with Kevin, and I

promise no more blackberries." He held out his hand, and she reluctantly accepted it.

He smiled and gave her an appreciative nod. "You know, there's something I've been wanting to ask you."

"I'm almost afraid to ask. What?"

"How come a beautiful woman like you is single?"

She shrugged. "Who said I'm single?"

He shook his head. "Okay, that's the last assumption I'm making." He pulled up to the B and B and jumped out of the truck.

Before Tayler could say anything else, Rollin was standing outside holding the door for her.

He looked down at his watch. "Just in time for lunch." Then he reached in and swept her up in his arms again.

Tayler started to protest. "I can—"

"I'm taking you to the porch. Can't have you cutting your feet, now can I?"

She relaxed in his arms. "I guess not."

Chapter 6

Come Thursday morning, Tayler surprised Rollin when she walked into the dining room for breakfast. He looked up from his newspaper and arched a brow.

"Good morning," she said.

"Well, good morning to you, too." He folded the paper and set it on the table. "I didn't expect you this early."

"I didn't want to try my luck eating at Donita's again. So I guess that means I've got a truck ride ahead of me."

The kitchen door opened and Rita walked into the room carrying a platter of eggs and bacon. "Tayler! Good morning."

"Morning, Rita."

Rita set the platter in the center of the dining room table. "You're just in time for breakfast, and I didn't have to send Rollin up for you."

Tayler smiled as she took a seat. "No, I won't be missing breakfast again. Let's just say I learned my lesson."

Rita placed her hands on her hips and smiled. "Nothing's wrong with Donita's. The cook's just not as good as I am."

"You can say that again." Rollin interjected. "I've got the best cook in the county."

"I don't know about that." Rita turned around and headed back into the kitchen. "Rollin, grab y'all some plates."

Rollin walked over to the buffet and took out two plates. Tayler tried not to stare, but the view of his rear was so enticing. He looked like a calendar model for *Hot Farmers Monthly.* His worn but fitted black jeans hugged his thighs and showed off his nice round…

"Tayler?"

She blinked when she realized Rollin was talking to her. "I'm sorry, what did you say?"

"I asked if you mind me joining you for breakfast."

"Of course not."

Seconds later, Rita returned with another platter of food. "Breakfast is served."

An hour after breakfast Kevin sat in the truck talking on his cell phone, while Tayler strolled through the pear trees trying to decipher what needed to be picked. She'd thought at least Kevin would help her, but she should have known better. She picked up a good-looking pear from the ground and put it in the small basket she'd gotten from the back of the truck.

"That one's a little too ripe."

She turned around, surprised to see Rollin.

"I thought you might need some help."

She let out a deep sigh. Hell, yeah, she needed help, but she wouldn't have ever admitted it. "I don't have Miss Barbara's assistance, but I'm doing okay." She looked into her basket.

"Let me see what you've got so far." He took the basket and looked around inside.

"Don't think I can pick fruit either, huh?" she asked.

He handed the basket back to her. "Sure you can. It's just like being in the grocery store. You wouldn't purchase a rotten pear, would you?"

He took a pear off the top and tossed it into a nearby compost receptacle.

"No, I wouldn't," she replied, looking after the bruised pear. "Hey, how did that get in there?"

He nodded toward the truck. "What's he doing?"

"Not helping me, that's for sure."

Rollin walked over to the truck and had a few words with Kevin before he pulled off.

"He's leaving us out here?" Tayler asked, pointing toward the departing truck.

"He'll be back. He sits around talking to his girl-friend too much."

"How old is he? He looks like he's still in high school."

Rollin laughed. "He's been out of school for a couple of years now. He just looks young. That's what good country living does for you." He pointed beyond the pear trees. "Come on, the squash is down here. You've got enough pears."

"Well, how old are you?" she asked as she followed him. "That is, if you don't mind me asking. You only look a couple of years out of high school yourself."

"I'm thirty-two, and you? That is, if you don't mind me asking."

"Not at all. I'm thirty-six."

He stopped and looked her up and down with a big grin on his face. "Damn, you seriously don't look thirty-six."

"Thank you. And let me congratulate you on all your accomplishments at such a young age. I know it's a lot of hard work."

"Thanks. It is, but I'm not afraid of hard work. Inherited that from my pops. He started all of this, I'm just trying to take it to the next level."

"So you grew up working the farm as a young boy?"

"Yep, worked every morning before I left for school." He walked over to a group of low shrubs and reached for her basket again. "Come here and let me show you how to select squash."

She followed him over to the vines.

"Put your basket down. There's an art to picking squash that you have to respect."

"You have to respect picking squash?" she asked, looking at him as if he was crazy. *Is he serious?*

"Of course you do. You respect the land and treat it with love. It's like a relationship. We have a mutual respect for one another."

"You and the squash?" she asked, arching a brow.

"I know it may sound a little strange to you." He knelt down and gently pulled and poked the yellow squash before placing it into her basket. "It should be tender to the touch."

She tried not to laugh but couldn't help herself. "I'm picturing you caressing squash—in a respectful way, of course."

"Oh, you got jokes. I'm trying to teach you something and you're laughing at me."

She stopped laughing. "Okay, I'm sorry. I didn't realize I was being schooled."

"That's right, come on down here and pick a few yourself."

She squatted next to him where the vines ran along the ground and followed his lead.

"That's right, pull it by the neck, then use your fingernail and press gently about a half inch below the stem. If you can make an indent, it's ready. You don't want it if it's too tough. But we harvest them when they're young, so all of these should be good." His velvety-smooth voice was a sharp contrast to the roughness of his hands.

She grabbed another one and unintentionally inserted her fingernail right into the vegetable.

"Not like that." He took Tayler's hand in his and guided her to another squash. "Let me show you."

They took hold of another squash.

"Push with your fingernail like this." He guided her finger through the touch. "See how soft that is?"

Every nerve in every finger came alive at his unintentional caress. A flush of heat surged through her body that set off a warning alarm in her head. She looked up into his eyes while his hand stroked hers over the squash.

"There you go—you're getting the hang of it. Make sure it's not too soft or too hard. A little firmness is good."

The sensual reference was too much. She yanked her hand away from his and fell backward onto her butt.

"Hey, you okay?" Rollin asked as he helped her stand up.

Embarrassed as hell, she brushed herself off and then kept repeating, "I'm fine, I'm fine. Really, I'm okay."

He grinned and looked down at her. "You look a little flushed."

She fanned herself. "It's the heat. Boy, is it hot out here." She looked down into her basket and knew she'd never look at squash the same.

The truck came barreling back up the road, kicking dust everywhere as it pulled to a screeching halt close to them.

Kevin rolled down the window. "Rollin, we're runnin' late for the market."

Rollin dropped his squash into Tayler's basket and looked at his watch. "Damn, I lost track of time. Is everything ready?" he asked Kevin.

"Everything's loaded and heading on over. I was just waiting on you to call me." Kevin held up his cell phone.

Rollin took Tayler's basket. "Here, let's put this in the back of the truck. We need to get going."

Rollin opened the door and helped Tayler climb up into the truck. Immediately, she realized Kevin's truck wasn't as big as Rollin's. She scooted over as Rollin eased in next to her.

He swung his left arm behind her back to rest on the seat and closed the door. She crossed her ankles, trying to keep her thigh to herself, but it was impossible. Kevin took off, turning the truck around so fast, Tayler almost landed in Rollin's lap.

She hoped Kevin would drive her back to the house

since she was practically wedged into Rollin. However, the truck pulled out from the fields and headed in the opposite direction.

"Uh, excuse me. Would you mind dropping me off at the B and B first?" she asked, looking from Kevin to Rollin.

"Sorry, but you're gonna have to ride to market with us this morning," Rollin said, and then pulled out his cell phone when it rang.

Tayler looked at Kevin. "Is he serious?"

"Uh-huh, but we'll only be gone a couple of hours. The farmers' market is only open Thursdays from eight until noon."

An hour later, Tayler handed a cute little girl with long plaits and the chubbiest cheeks she'd ever seen a bag of apples. She handed the mother the change.

"Are you new?" the child's mother asked.

Tayler opened her mouth to respond and stopped short of saying, *hell, no, I got roped into this.* "No, I'm only helping out for a little while this morning."

"Oh, that's why I haven't seen you around town."

"I'm visiting."

"You're visiting Rollin?"

What's with all the nosy questions?

"Bernice, are you over here harassing the help?" Kevin asked as he walked up.

The woman laughed. "Of course not, I just wanted to introduce myself." She offered a hand to Tayler. "I'm Bernice Eversole."

Tayler accepted her hand. "Hi, Bernice, I'm Tayler Carter."

"Nice meeting you. Are you visiting Corra or Rollin?"

Tayler smiled. "Neither. I'm actually a guest at the B and B."

Tayler's mother would have called Bernice thick, or big-boned. She was an attractive woman but had the worst weave Tayler had ever seen. Her piercing eyes searched behind Tayler in the direction of Rollin, who was helping a man load a bushel of green beans onto his truck.

Bernice grinned. "That really is some working farm y'all got over there. You even put the guests on the vegetable stand."

"Bernice, you know we're like family at Coleman House," Rollin stressed as he walked up and placed his arm around Tayler's shoulders. "Tayler's the newest member of the family."

The look on Bernice's face matched the shock on Tayler's. Rollin's touch always did something to her no matter where she was. She smiled as he pulled her close enough to inhale his woodsy scent. His lips moved so she knew he said something, but being this close to him again shut off a piece of her brain.

"Yeah, I see," Bernice said and cocked a brow.

The minute Bernice left, Tayler gathered her senses and slid away from Rollin. She looked from him to Kevin. Each one had a big grin on his face.

"What was that all about?" she asked.

"I'm sorry. I hope you don't mind us having a little fun at your expense. Bernice has to know everybody and everything."

"And she'd like to get to know Rollin a lot better, too," Kevin added.

Rollin shook his head. "It's not like that."

"Oh, here comes another one of his girlfriends." Kevin walked off as another young woman approached.

"Hey, Rollin," she called out in a singsong voice.

Rollin cleared his throat. "Mornin', Cassie."

"Mama sent me over to see if you had any tomatoes left."

Young, hot and ready for trouble was how Tayler would have described Cassie in her shorts and high heels.

"We sure do. Right down there where Kevin's at." Rollin pointed to the other end of their area of the farmers' market.

"You know I never did learn how to pick good tomatoes." Cassie chuckled while looking at Tayler. "You know how it is, girl. I just get mine from the IGA grocery. But Mama likes the ones from Coleman's farm."

Tayler smiled.

"Rollin, can you help me pick out some nice, firm but juicy tomatoes?" Cassie asked.

She bit the tip of her finger in a coy way that made Tayler roll her eyes. *Oh, my God.* Cassie's body language flirted with Rollin so hard Tayler felt like a voyeur. Rollin walked around the table. *How gullible. Men are so stupid*, Tayler thought.

"Kev." Rollin motioned for Kevin. "I'll tell you what, Cassie, Kevin will help you pick out some tomatoes, and he'll get your mama a few green ones. I know how she likes fried green tomatoes." With his arm around Cassie's shoulder, he handed her off to Kevin, who hustled over with a big smile on his face.

"Well… I guess so," she mumbled, walking away.

Rollin came back around the table, shaking his head.

"Looks like you're pretty popular around here. A single brother with not one but two businesses. I see the ladies throw themselves at you," Tayler said.

He shook his head before responding. "That's a child."

"She has all the makings of a woman, that's for sure. What about Bernice? She's not a child," Tayler added with a playful smile.

Rollin took a deep breath and stroked his goatee. Every time he struck a pose she got a tingle in the pit of her stomach. *Damn, he's fine.*

Rollin started rearranging the baskets of pears. "Can we change the subject?" he asked without looking at Tayler.

Two women walked by with broad smiles and waved. "Hi, Rollin."

He gave them a quick nod. "Mornin', ladies."

Tayler crossed her arms and laughed. "Yeah, I can see it now. You smile at them with those big dimples of yours and you can have any woman in town."

He shook his head and laughed. "My day starts at five a.m. and usually doesn't end until after dinner. I don't have time for a woman right now. My business is my lady."

"Sure it is."

"Besides," Rollin continued, "I'm trying to get into some bigger markets, like Whole Foods."

Tayler nodded. "Then you won't have to stand out here selling at a farmers' market, huh?"

"I don't have to be out here now, Kevin can handle

this. But I enjoy talking to people who eat our produce to see what they have to say. It's my market research. I bring food to the people. Not everyone wants to come out and pick their own food."

She held up her hand. "Amen."

A few more customers stopped by to purchase vegetables. Once everyone left, Tayler picked their conversation right back up.

"So, why can't you get into Whole Foods?"

"It's a long story, but basically we need more money to expand in order to meet their demand. Holding onto the land and the B and B takes a lot of money."

"Did you ever think about selling it all and leaving Danville?"

"Never. This is home. I came back here after college, and I don't ever plan on leaving. It's a nice town."

"Looks like it."

"I'll tell you what, after we leave I can give you the grand tour. I'll show you my town, and then you'll see why I love it so much."

She smiled. "Sure."

"Well, if it isn't Tayler Carter."

Tayler and Rollin turned around as Officer Greg approached the table.

"So, we meet again." He extended his hand. "Good morning."

"Good morning, Officer Greg." Tayler accepted his hand.

"Please, call me Greg."

"What's up, man?" Rollin reached out to shake Greg's hand.

"Nothing much. I saw you guys over here and

thought I'd say hello and see if Tayler is up for that tour I promised her."

Tayler and Rollin exchanged glances.

Chapter 7

Tayler turned to Greg, then back to Rollin, and waited on him to say something—anything.

"Unless you've already been on a tour, as part of your stay at the B and B," Greg said, looking from Tayler to Rollin.

Rollin shook his head. "Nope, not part of the package."

She couldn't believe Rollin was going to leave her hanging out there like that. "Actually, Greg, I'm kinda busy today."

Greg took a step back and then picked up a pear to examine it. "Yeah, I see they've put you to work. Rollin, I didn't know things were so bad you'd put the guest to work," he said.

Rollin crossed his arms. "Who said things were bad at all?" he asked.

Tayler heard a hint of annoyance creep into Rollin's voice.

Greg placed the pear back on the stack. "Well, I heard you've had a lot of vacancies. And with school about to start back, you'll probably lose some of your workforce."

"I don't know where you heard that. We're doing okay. I'll lose two guys when school starts, but that's all. And Tayler—"

He glanced over at her, and she could see his face hardening.

"She's only here because I didn't have time to run her back to the house after we ran an errand."

Greg flashed Rollin a cold smile, then turned back to Tayler.

"Thanks, Greg, but I'm gonna hang around the B and B the rest of the day."

Greg shrugged as his mouth turned downward. "Well, if you change your mind, you've got my card."

"Yes, I do."

"You folks have a good day. I'll be waiting for that call."

Tayler nodded and smiled as he backed away.

"Later, man," Rollin added, then turned to Tayler. "Sure you didn't want to take him up on his offer instead of mine?"

She crossed her arms. "If I did I wouldn't be standing here." Rollin winked and gave her a smile that set off those sexy dimples. She wished he hadn't done that—it made her stomach do flip-flops.

"Come on, let's sell some strawberries. We've got customers."

She turned around as a few people approached the stand.

After they returned to the B and B, Tayler had a long hot shower and then poured herself a tall glass of Rita's tea. She then found a nice quiet spot in the library to read.

She now realized she had to put as much distance between her and Rollin as possible. Any woman in her right mind would be attracted to him, but she didn't want to be. In less than a week's time she already had the hots for the guy. What was wrong with her? She didn't usually let herself get this worked up over any man. But then, Rollin wasn't just any man.

She opened her book and forced herself to read. This attraction she had to Rollin was going to stop right now.

A couple of hours later, she heard the sound of Rollin's work boots coming down the hallway toward the library. He cradled his cell phone between his ear and shoulder while he mumbled, "Uh-huh," a few times into the phone. He held the cell out and quickly pulled his T-shirt up his back and over his head with one hand.

Tayler's eyes widened but she couldn't have said anything if she'd wanted to. *Oh, my God!* If she wasn't looking at a perfect specimen of a man, one didn't exist. He looked like chiseled chocolate.

He rubbed the shirt across his chest and under his arms before pitching it into a nearby chair. He didn't notice her curled up in the corner with her feet tucked underneath her as he walked straight to the desk on the opposite side of the room and pulled open the drawer.

Tayler's head tilted as her eyes traced the muscles in his back. Not an ounce of fat. Farmwork did a body good.

Afraid he might catch her staring, she returned to her book. She could hear him fumbling around in a desk drawer, and he still hadn't noticed her. She stole another peek and wondered what having his big triceps wrapped around her at night might feel like. The last time she'd shared her bed with a man escaped her. She bit her bottom lip.

"Rollin!"

Tayler jumped and turned toward the door where Rita's husband, Wallace, stood nodding his head toward her. Rollin whipped around and noticed her for the first time.

"Hold on a minute," he said into the phone. "I'm sorry, I didn't know you were in here," he explained as he closed the drawer.

Her eyes locked on his chest as her teeth let go of her lip. Then she turned into a stuttering idiot. "I... I started to say something, but, uh, you were on the phone." She quickly pulled her feet out from underneath her and stood up. She picked up her glass of iced tea.

"Boy, go put a shirt on," Wallace said.

Tayler held her hand up. "Don't do that on my account."

After a quick glance from Rollin to Wallace, she realized what that sounded like. "I mean, I'm leaving anyway." She eased toward the door. "I should be outside on such a beautiful day. I'll let you guys continue to do whatever you were about to do in here." She scooted past Wallace, who seemed very amused by her. "Excuse me."

"Don't let us run you off," Wallace added.

Tayler turned around. "No, you're not. I could use the fresh air." Unable to resist, she took one last peek at Rollin as he maneuvered his discarded T-shirt over his head, and she stumbled back over the rug in the hallway.

Wallace reached out to catch her. "You okay?" he asked.

She spilled some tea but managed to hold onto everything else. "Oh, God, I'm sorry. I spilled tea on the rug."

"Don't worry about that. You just be careful. Wouldn't want you to fall and hurt yourself. The boy's insurance ain't paid up."

Tayler wiped at the tea on her pant leg and looked up at Rollin, who shook his head laughing.

"I get it," she said, smiling. "You don't want a lawsuit."

Wallace grinned even bigger. "You got it."

"Trust me, I wouldn't do that. I'm gonna go out back and sit in the garden for a while. You sure you don't want me to clean this up?" she asked, once more before leaving.

"Don't worry about it, I'll get it." Rollin walked around them and down the hall toward his private quarters.

"Well, okay," she said to Wallace before leaving.

"Enjoy the sunshine, pretty lady."

She glanced back over her shoulder. "I will." *Big flirt.*

In the garden, she chose a wrought-iron love seat surrounded by the magnificent aroma of flowers. She cracked her book open and continued to read. Halfway through another chapter she heard what sounded like thunder coming from the wraparound porch.

Tayler looked up as Corra's children jumped off the porch and ran out in the direction of the barn.

"Don't get in Rollin's way. Did y'all hear me?" Corra shouted.

"Yes, ma'am," they called out.

Tayler waved when Corra looked her way.

"Just who I was looking for," Corra said and walked over.

Tayler pointed to herself. "Who, me?"

"Yes, you. Remember I wanted to talk to you about helping down at the school with our fund-raiser to purchase computers? That is, if you aren't too busy around here."

Corra took the wrought-iron chair next to Tayler. "My brother isn't working you too hard, is he?"

"No, not at all. I'm actually beginning to enjoy the morning truck rides. It's amazing what a little time in the country can do for you."

Corra crossed her legs and took a deep breath. "Yep, a couple of weeks out here can transform you. We see it all the time. People arrive all tense, but they leave so relaxed."

"That's what I'm hoping for."

Corra twisted around in her seat to face Tayler. "So, Rollin was telling me that you're a vice president at your job, is that right?"

"I'm vice president of strategic alliance, not the whole company."

"That sounds interesting. I bet you're good at persuading people to do things for you."

Tayler closed her book. "One could say that. How can I help you?"

Corra crossed her legs. "Well, we could use help soliciting items for the silent auction. I created the pitch we're using, but it could stand to be more persuasive. Can you help with that?"

"Sure, I have plenty of experience in that area. You know, Nicole and I have a nonprofit organization called the Color of Success, and we're always soliciting for sponsorships."

"Cool. So what do you guys do, exactly?"

"We give empowerment workshops to young women all over the US. Our goal is to educate, empower and inspire young women. We teach them about having confidence and self-respect."

"You and Nicole travel all over to do that?"

"We do. We bring in women from the community to discuss personal challenges they've faced and overcome in their lives. It's a wonderful program."

"It sounds like it. We need something like that around here. How did you get started?"

"Fortunately, my job affords me the luxury of traveling the world and meeting people from all walks of life. I was invited to be the keynote speaker at a women's empowerment conference in Los Angeles years ago, and the work they were doing moved me so that I wanted to start my own organization. However, at the time I was traveling and working so much I didn't have the time. But after sharing the experience with Nicole and discovering we were of like minds, she went to work setting everything up and the rest is history. It's a labor of love."

Corra held a hand to her chest. "Man, I would love to do something like that. Maybe while you're here you can come speak to the young women's group at my church? Or at the school."

Tayler laughed. "I'll see what I can do."

"Too bad I didn't know about that earlier—I would have asked you to speak at the ceremony. How much do you charge?"

Tayler know her speaking fee was more than they would be able to pay. "I'll tell you what, you let me know when and where and I'll speak to them for free."

Corra's eyes widened. "You'd do that for us?"

Tayler pressed her lips together and smiled. "Why not."

"Girl, let me get up from here before I intrude on your vacation anymore."

"It's not an intrusion. I love speaking to young women. I want them to know they're worthy of going after their dreams."

"You've just inspired me so much just now. We have a committee meeting tonight if you can make it. We'll go over all the details of the silent auction and the ceremony being held at the end of the fall festival in about a month."

"Just let me know where to show up."

Tayler liked Corra, and helping with the fund-raiser would be a perfect way to get away from the house and Rollin. She didn't trust herself around that man. He was her accident waiting to happen.

One week into her vacation, and Tayler had a new friend in Nicole's cousin Corra. Tayler helped her perfect the sales pitch before they rode around town collecting items for the silent auction. After the last stop, they headed back to Corra's house in her gently used Toyota Corolla.

"Girl, you have to tell me where you got those sandals. I can't stand up in heels like that, let alone walk around all day in them. Your feet don't hurt?" Corra asked.

Tayler looked down at her Stuart Weitzman wedges.

"No, they're actually very comfortable. They were a gift."

"Now that's what I call a present. You must have been good to somebody to get those," Corra teased.

"They were an *I'm sorry* gift. You can tell how much dirt a man's done by the size of the gift when he gets back in town."

Corra laughed. "I wouldn't know anything about that. The best gift I've ever received are those two kids of mine."

"I'm sure they'd beat a pair of shoes any day," Tayler added.

Corra sighed. "Yeah, I guess you're right. I hope today didn't bore you to death."

"Not at all. I enjoyed myself. I met some really cool people and learned a lot about life in the country. I'll admit those first few days were a little rough, but I can get used to this slower pace."

"That's a nice way to put it. We call it Dullsville, but it's my home and I can't bring myself to leave."

"Why would you want to?" Tayler asked.

"Oh, I don't know. Maybe to find a man who'll buy me expensive shoes and love my kids. Those men don't live around here."

"What, no old high school sweetheart?"

"Girlfriend, been there, done that, got two kids to show for it. I haven't seen my ex-husband in over two years. He moved to California without looking back."

"Men can be dogs," Tayler blurted out.

"You can say that again," Corra added. "Except for

my brother, who's the sweetest guy I know. There need to be more men like him in this town."

"I gather he's a hot commodity?"

Corra smirked. "The women in this town have been on him like white on rice. Thankfully, he's more focused on the family business than some of these scallywags."

"He doesn't have a girlfriend?" Tayler asked.

"Nope. He dated a woman over in Bullet County for a while, but that didn't last."

"Do you ever work at the farm?"

"Me, naw. I've helped out from time to time when they're in a pinch, but Rollin handles everything. He has a business degree from Morehouse College in Atlanta. Although this isn't what he'd planned to do with it."

Arriving at her house, Corra backed into the driveway and popped the trunk. "Let's pile everything in the basement."

Tayler grabbed a large gift basket and followed Corra inside the house. The split-level country-style home was nicely decorated and reminded Tayler of her room at the B and B.

Tayler could hear the children and noise from a television as she followed Corra downstairs. At the bottom of the stairs she walked into a large den, and who was sitting in front of the television with the children but Rollin. She hadn't seen his truck outside. He did a double take after he noticed her.

"Score!" Jamie yelled.

Rollin turned back to the screen. "Dude, you beat me again."

Jamie danced around the den. "I always do, Uncle Rollin."

"That you do." Rollin set the controller down. "Let's take a break, little buddy, and see if your mother needs any help."

Before Tayler could make it across the room, Rollin reached out for the gift basket. "I'm surprised to see you here," he said.

"Imagine my surprise," Tayler said, with a stiff smile.

Rollin and Jamie volunteered to go get everything else, while Tayler found a nice comfortable spot at the end of the sofa, where Corra's daughter, Katie, kept her company.

Minutes later, everyone was in the den when Corra announced, "Okay, guys, I've got the game plan for tomorrow. We're pairing up in twos again because it's more effective that way. I'm going to hit the local hospital with Sharon. And I've got you two—" she pointed from Rollin to Tayler "—down for the strip mall out on Bicknell Road."

Tayler's jaw dropped before she turned to Rollin.

Chapter 8

Tayler stood up so fast, she almost knocked little Katie down. "Uh, Corra, I don't know about tomorrow."

Rollin came to Tayler's rescue, knowing how his sister had a habit of manipulating people into doing anything she wanted. "Yeah, Corra, the market's all day Saturday, and after that I—"

"Oh, come on, Rollin, you know Kevin can run that stand on Saturday. This is for the kids, man, your niece and nephew. Don't you want them to have computers, too?" she pleaded.

"They have one up in their room. I brought it last Christmas."

Corra stomped her foot. "I'm talkin' 'bout at school. They need computers in the classroom. The effort we put in now will pay off big in the long run."

Rollin looked at Tayler to gauge her reaction to Corra's ranting. He was used to her but didn't want Tayler to feel put upon. "I'm sure Tayler has other plans for tomorrow."

"Yes, I want to check out an antique shop I saw today."

"Girl, you can do that anytime." The telephone rang and Corra excused herself to go answer it, with Katie in tow. "Y'all figure things out. I'll be right back."

Alone with Tayler, Rollin felt the need to apologize. "Hey, I'm sorry you got roped into this. Don't worry about tomorrow. Corra has other folk working on the fund-raiser who can pitch in. She took advantage of your kindness all day today. I think she's forgotten you're not just Nicole's friend, but a guest of ours."

"That's okay, I really don't mind helping," Tayler said, crossing her arms. "It's just that, uh, I don't think her plans for *us* working together are such a good idea."

Rollin lifted his chin while revisiting a mental picture of him carrying her in his arms. That moment had caused his nerve endings to tingle, and set off a desire to touch and explore her body. Not only did Corra need to remember Tayler was a guest, but he had to remind himself as well. "Yeah, you might be right."

Corra reentered the room. "So, what did you guys work out while I was gone?"

Instead of spending less time with Rollin, Tayler found herself riding around Danville bright and early with a man whose touch had the power to set her body on fire. Being in such close proximity with Rollin did a number on Tayler's imagination. Every time he smiled at her, she could visualize his bare chest and her hands exploring his rock-hard chiseled abs.

She bit her fingernail and stared out the window at the fields and fields of deep green grass and knew then why they called Kentucky the bluegrass state.

"This shouldn't take too long," Rollin said.

Tayler swallowed and turned away from the scenic view. "Let's hope not. I still want to check out that antique shop."

"I've got a lot of stuff to do myself. If Corra weren't my sister, she wouldn't have been able to talk me into this. How did she talk you into helping out, anyway?"

Tayler took a deep breath and sighed. "She just asked. It's not like I'm busy doing anything." *Other than trying to keep my distance from you.* "So I'm happy to help raise funds."

He pulled into a parking spot at one end of the mall and killed the engine. "Well, it's time for you to do your thing."

She grabbed her pitch, although she didn't really need it, and opened the truck door. Before she could climb down, Rollin was there offering his hand. She accepted it and stepped out in her heels, trying not to bump into him and possibly ignite a flame. But she stepped right into that citrus and woodsy smell of his that made her want to snuggle up next to him.

The first stop was a gift shop that sold everything Kentucky related. The owner, a short, heavyset white woman, was overjoyed to see Rollin. "Well, lookie here, I haven't seen you in months. How's everything over at the B and B? Honey, you look just like your daddy, you know that?"

Rollin blushed and spent the next fifteen minutes updating her about the goings-on at the B and B.

Minutes later, they did the same thing at the Family Dollar Store, the hardware store and then the cleaner's.

The friendship Rollin seemed to have with everyone around town impressed Tayler. Everyone expressed how proud they were of him and Corra before expressing an interest in who Tayler was.

"Your sister said you were hot stuff in this town," Tayler said once they were outside again.

Rollin laughed. "I don't believe Corra said that about me."

"Maybe not in those exact words, but that's what she said."

"These people knew my pops and what he was trying to build with the farm. They're just glad I didn't sell it when my parents died, that's all."

"Yeah, right. Like the women at the farmer's market on Thursday? Admit it, you're Mr. Danville, local heartthrob," she teased. Spending this time with Rollin wasn't as bad as she'd thought it was going to be. So far, she'd managed to keep her hormones in check.

"You're enjoying this, aren't you?" he asked.

Tayler laughed. "Hey, I'm trying to get some donations here, but you keep stealing my thunder with your long-winded conversations. So far, we've gotten three promises for gift certificates out of five people."

"Maybe it's your technique."

She stopped and placed a hand on her hip. "My technique! I don't think so. Yesterday Corra and I managed to get over five hundred dollars' worth of donations."

"Hey, I can't compete with two beautiful women.

One look at you and Corra, and I'm not surprised you didn't get enough money to purchase the computers outright."

Tayler tried not to blush. "Thank you, but don't try to change the subject, Mr. Danville."

He shook his head, then motioned for her to follow him. "Come on, let's get out of here. I've had enough of this."

Tayler climbed back in the truck, exhausted from listening and talking so much.

"This isn't going to be easy, is it?" she asked, looking down the strip at the other shops they hadn't made it to.

Rollin started the truck and peered over at her. "Nope, but I can't take any more today. At this rate we won't finish anytime soon." He glanced down at his watch. "I need to catch up with Rita before she leaves today. She wasn't looking too good this morning."

He sat his cell phone in the middle console of the truck and it rang immediately, as if on cue. He picked it up. After a couple of *uh huh*s, and "take care of yourself," he hung up. "Rita won't be back this evening—she's got a cold."

"That's too bad. I hope she feels better soon."

He glanced out the window. "Yeah, me, too." Then he turned to her. "Looks like I'm your cook for tonight."

"Can you cook?" she asked.

He tilted his head toward her. "What do you think?"

She shrugged. "I don't know. Let's see, you're a businessman, a farmer, an innkeeper, and now you're telling me you're a chef." She couldn't believe this gorgeous man was so amazing.

He smiled. "I'm no Emeril, but I can handle dinner."

"A real Renaissance man," she said with a smile.

He chuckled and glanced her way with a glint in his eyes and the sexiest smile she'd ever seen. There went that tingle in the pit of her stomach again. This time it traveled lower when she thought of them having dinner alone tonight. She turned to look out the window. *Lord, help me.*

Once they reached the house, Tayler walked into her room and closed the door behind her. *God, why are you punishing me with this man? I need to get away from him.* She closed her eyes and said a silent prayer for strength before she kicked off her sandals. If she was going to get through this month without jumping his bones, she needed help. She quickly jumped out of her clothes and into the shower.

She changed outfits three times, never satisfied with her look. "What am I doing?" she stopped and asked herself. "I'm getting prepped for dinner like I'm going on a date." She looked at herself in the mirror and decided on a pair of jeans, a sleeveless top and her sneakers.

"Not too revealing," she said. Finally satisfied with herself, she went to see if she could help with dinner.

Tayler found Rollin in the kitchen going through the drawers. He'd turned the radio on to the only R&B station you could pick up in the county.

She stood in the doorway for a few seconds, admiring the view. A good-looking man who also knew his way around the kitchen really turned her on. If her girlfriends could see this, they'd be standing in line for a chance to be alone with him like this. She cleared her throat.

* * *

Rollin turned around to see Tayler rub her palms together. "Do you need any help?" she asked.

He shook his head. "I got this." He quickly turned away from her so she couldn't see the desire in his eyes. She had on a pair of tight-fitting jeans and a T-shirt that fit snugly around her breasts. He'd be damned if anything that woman put on didn't do a number on him. He forced himself yet again to remember she was a guest.

He glanced back over his shoulder to where she stood looking around the kitchen as though she needed something to do. "I'll tell you what, why don't you grab that bottle of wine from the bottom shelf of the refrigerator."

When Tayler walked over, opened the refrigerator and bent over, she caught his eye. He arched a brow at her beautiful backside. She closed the door and before he could turn back to the stove she caught him staring at her. For the first time, he wished they had a house full of guests. He silently hoped Rita's cold was nothing more than a twenty-four-hour bug.

"What are you preparing?" she asked.

"Lucky for us, Rita marinated some chicken breasts and vegetables.

"This is the first time I've ever stayed at a bed-and-breakfast. I wasn't aware they served dinner until Nicole told me you guys did."

"We didn't always, but more and more guests began inquiring about it, since we're an organic farm. So, about a year ago, we incorporated dinner into the package. Rita loves to cook, so she welcomed the idea."

"That was a smart move."

When I Fall in Love

He shrugged. "It's a little more work, but it made us stand out from the other B and Bs around the area."

"I have to admit I'm starting to enjoy the truck rides. It gives me time to think."

"I'm glad to see you're coming around. Watch and see, before you leave, we'll have you driving a tractor."

"Oh, no," Tayler said with a laugh. "That'll never happen."

"Never say never. You are staying two months, right?"

"Well, that's up in the air. But I have no intention of mounting a tractor."

Rollin caught an image of Tayler mounting something, but it wasn't a tractor. He couldn't keep the silly grin off his face.

"What's so funny?" she asked.

He shook his head. "Nothing. I just had this picture of you on a tractor with your four-inch heels on." *And preferably nothing else.*

"You don't like high heels or something?"

"Look in that drawer next to you and grab the wine-bottle opener." He took the bottle from her. "I love a woman in high heels. They're sexy. They're just not for the farm." She handed him the opener. "Wineglasses are over there in the last cabinet on the left."

Tayler found them and set two wineglasses in front of him and stood there with her arms crossed. He poured each of them a glass before leaning against the counter.

"I'll give it to you, though, you have a mean shoe game. A woman with expensive taste." He took a sip of wine. "I bet all your vacation is missing is a spa and a Starbucks."

She picked up her glass. "You know, I think I'll wait in the library. Please let me know when dinner is ready."

She strutted across the kitchen with her nose turned up, which turned Rollin on. "Hold on now, don't leave." Tayler stopped at the kitchen door and looked back over her shoulder. This woman was getting under his skin so bad he just wanted to kiss her and get it over with.

"Look, beautiful women such as yourself take vacations to the Caribbean or somewhere with spas and beaches—any place but a farm on the outskirts of Danville, Kentucky. You're not my typical guest, that's all, and I know you expected more. But stay and keep me company. I promise to keep my foot out of my mouth the rest of the night."

As she turned around, a slow smile managed to find its way to her face. "That might be hard, since you do it so well."

"Touché. I deserved that."

She strolled back over to the kitchen island and sat on a bar stool. Once she set her glass down he poured more wine.

"Thank you," Tayler murmured.

"You're welcome." Everything this evening was taking longer than Rollin anticipated. He had paperwork to do that he should have worked on earlier, but there was always tomorrow. He hadn't met a woman like Tayler in a long time and couldn't get enough of her company.

Tayler sipped her wine and asked herself why she'd come back to keep him company. She needed to be in the library waiting on dinner, or sitting on the front porch, enjoying a nice breeze. Sitting in the kitchen watching him cook was more like a date.

"How's the wine?" he asked.

"It's good."

Neither one of them said anything for a few minutes. Only the sizzle of the food cooking could be heard. She looked around trying to find a conversation piece to break the awkward silence.

She read the label on the wine bottle. "Castle Hill." Is this organic wine, too?"

"Of course. It's a white wine from Versailles, Kentucky, and the chicken is free-range. A little more expensive, but worth it. How has your food been so far?"

"Everything has been amazing."

"Food free of chemical fertilizers and pesticides tastes better, plus it's better for you."

"It does a body good, huh?" she asked and took another sip of wine.

Propped against the counter with his arms crossed, Rollin nodded. She struggled not to undress him with her eyes again.

"I don't know, you tell me," he said with a smile.

She cleared her throat. "You're the one who grew up on it, not me. My mother used to stop at the closest fast food joint on her way home most of the time. She wasn't exactly a cook."

"I didn't grow up eating organic. I learned about it in college." He turned around to check on the food but continued educating her about everything organic.

Tayler was impressed with his knowledge of soil erosion and how organic production reduced health risks like some cancers and other diseases. She listened and learned.

Once dinner was ready, they moved the conversation into the dining room. He'd already set the table for two.

"Man, today has been an education, that's for sure," she said.

"I told you this vacation is going to be an experience you'll never forget."

She laughed. "Oh, it's off to a good start."

Chapter 9

Tayler took her usual seat for dinner, while Rollin sat across from her.

After blessing the food, he surprised her when he asked, "So, how does your man feel about you coming down here alone?"

She stopped chewing. "What man?"

"Yesterday I asked why you were single and I believe your reply was, 'Who said I was single?'" he said, mimicking her voice.

She lowered her head and started eating. "Well," she said between swallows. "I didn't say I was seeing anybody. It's just that I never said I was single. You made an assumption."

"Okay, but you are single?"

She held her head up. "At the moment, yes I am."

"Mm-hmm," he said tasting his chicken.

"What's that supposed to mean?"

He shook his head. "Nothing."

Tayler hesitated for a moment, then asked, "How come you're single?"

He shrugged. "I haven't met the right woman yet."

"What? Mr. Danville can't find Mrs. Danville?" she asked teasingly.

"Okay, you can cut that out," he said, pointing at her with his fork.

"That's right." She snapped her fingers. "You're Mr. Morehouse."

He arched a brow. "How did you know I went there?"

She grinned and tilted her head.

"Corra," he concluded. "I should have known. So what all did she tell you?" he asked and continued eating.

"Only that you received your business degree from Morehouse in Atlanta, and then came back here to work. I'm wondering why, though? A degree from Morehouse should have landed you a good job in Atlanta."

"I pursued my degree to learn how to run a business, and that's what I do."

"Was that the plan, to run the farm?"

"No, but after my parents died, I knew this was where I needed to be."

"If you don't mind me asking, how did your parents die?"

"Car accident. They were hit by a drunk driver."

"Wow. I'm sorry for you loss."

"Thanks. I've always wanted my own business like my pops had. Ownership was really important to him, and I guess he instilled that in me. I wanted to be successful on my own. What about you?"

"I received my master's in business from Northwestern University. Basically, I wanted to be rich," she said with a shrug of her shoulders. "The plan was to climb the corporate ladder until I reached the ceiling. Then I'd write a bestseller about my struggle and make a fortune off the book and speaking engagements."

He stopped eating and laughed. "Wow, you had it all figured out, didn't you."

"Hey, don't laugh. That plan has worked for some folks. And they're no different than me. I've made it to a VP position and established myself as a popular keynote speaker on women's empowerment. Plus, I live a very comfortable life. Don't you want to be rich some day?"

"Baby, I already am in so many ways, just not financially."

She smiled and her pulse quickened after being addressed so affectionately by him. "I like that answer. Well, I'm still working on it."

He held up his wineglass. "Here's to Tayler being rich and happy."

She smiled and toasted with him.

"So, what's the next step in your plan?" he asked and continued to eat.

"I'm in line for a director's position, which I plan on getting."

He nodded. "You sound very driven and focused. I'm sure you'll be even more successful."

"Thank you. And as hard as you work, I'm sure you'll get into Whole Foods. But I hope you don't have to close the B and B in order to do it, because I see great potential here. But whatever you decide I'm sure it will be for the best."

Rollin shared a glance with her that said they understood one another.

Rollin saw more than a Barbie doll in Tayler tonight. She essentially wanted the same thing out of life that he did—success.

"Dinner was great, thank you," she said and pushed her plate aside.

"You're welcome. My mother would be proud."

"Was your mother a good cook?"

"The best. Her cooking is what made them decide to open their home to guests. My pops said she needed to share her talents with the world, or the little piece of the world that happened through Danville."

"Your parents sound like wonderful people."

"They were. They died too young."

Tayler reminded Rollin of his mother in some ways. Jean Coleman always dressed as if she were expecting company. She loved her high heels, and had to be the most stylish black woman in Danville.

"Who do you resemble, your mother or father?" Tayler asked.

"A little of both, but most people say my pops." Rollin stacked their plates and stood up. "Let me show you something."

Tayler stood and Rollin heard her footsteps as she followed behind him as he made his way to the library.

He walked over to the bookcase and pulled out a photo album. Tayler stood next to him as he placed the book on the desk and flipped it open. "Here's a picture of my mother that was taken a month before the accident."

She looked down at the picture and smiled. "You do look like your mother. You have her dimples."

"Yeah." He flipped the page. "That's my pops."

"Corra definitely looks like your father, but you have his eyes."

"Yeah."

Rollin closed the book, but not before Tayler glimpsed another picture of him.

"Hold on." She flipped the book back open. "Is that you?"

It was a picture of him in a basketball uniform showing off legs that used to send Danville schoolgirls into a frenzy.

"You don't want to see my high school team pictures."

"You played basketball?"

"Yep, and baseball." He tried to close the book again.

"Oh, no, you don't," she said laughing. "I've got to see these pictures."

A loud clap caught their attention.

Tayler jumped. "What was that?" she asked.

Rollin let go of the photo album. "I don't know," he said and walked out into the hall.

Tayler followed him.

He opened the front door to blackness and a rainstorm.

"I didn't know it was raining," Tayler said.

Rollin stepped out onto the porch, where one of the large white rockers lay on its side, and then pulled all of the chairs against the house.

"That's what we heard," he said. The minute he came back in the phone rang. He hurried into the kitchen to pick it up.

A flash of lightning streaked across the sky before a deep rumbling noise preceded a loud clap of thunder. Tayler hurried closely behind Rollin into the kitchen.

"I need to make a run," Rollin said.

"Now?" Tayler asked, wide-eyed.

"I need to help get some equipment inside the barn. I'll be right back."

Another flash of lightning followed by thunder that shook the house sent Tayler dashing back into the windowless library.

"Don't tell me you're afraid of a little storm?" he asked, following her.

"A little storm! Do you see what's going on out there? That's no *little* storm."

He laughed. "Did you bring a jacket?"

"Not a raincoat."

"I'll get you a jacket and you can ride out with me."

"Oh, I don't think so. Who in their right mind runs out into a storm?"

"Want to stay here, then?"

Another flash of lightning shone through the glass around the front door.

"Where's the jacket?" she asked and trailed Rollin down the hall toward his private family quarters.

He realized that this was the first time she'd been beyond the reception desk. They passed an office and several other closed doors, which were bedrooms. He opened a closet door and took out a big ugly yellow jacket and handed it to her.

"Here, put this on. It'll keep you dry."

She pulled the jacket on and snapped it up to the neck. Rollin grabbed a dark green jacket for himself and put it on. He then led the way through the kitchen to the back door, where he grabbed a big flashlight. A loud clap of thunder greeted them as he opened the door.

Tayler squealed and then put her hand over her mouth.

Rollin closed the door and turned around. "Maybe you should stay here."

"No! Not by myself. The girl left alone in the house is always the one who gets killed. I'm going with you."

Grinning, he shook his head before he reached up and pulled her hood on. "Come on."

They ran out to the truck, where Rollin opened the door and quickly helped Tayler in. Once he drove off, the heavy rain obstructed the view so much so that he could barely see where he was going. But it didn't take long before he pulled up to the barn, where two of his farm hands were quickly getting equipment out of the rain.

"I'll be right back," Rollin said.

Tayler grabbed him by the arm and shook her head. "Don't leave me in here by myself. If the killer doesn't get her in the house, he pulls her out of the truck."

He shook his head. "You've been watching too many movies."

"Whatever," she said and pulled her hood on.

They jumped out and ran inside the barn. Tayler stood back and watched as Rollin and his employees carried pieces of heavy equipment into the barn. Buckets of water dropped from the sky now, and they worked quicker to get things tied down. Once finished, his guys ran from the barn to their late-model truck and took off.

"You okay?" he asked when he walked over to Tayler.

"Yeah, I'm good." She nodded.

The sky lit up and Tayler jumped from the counter she was leaning against right into Rollin's arms.

Laughing, he wrapped her arms around her. "You must not be living right if you're that afraid of lightning."

"Lightning strikes are deadly. You should know that."

"No more than riding in a car or taking a plane. You don't have to be this afraid. Did you have a bad experience or something?"

She pulled back and looked up into his eyes. "No, but my mother was always afraid of storms and I guess... I guess it just—" She seemed to lose her train of thought as she stared up at his face. "It just sort of... uh...rubbed off on me."

Rollin's arms wrapped around her body felt warm and comforting. He knew he needed to pull away from her, but he couldn't. Lost in the deep pools of her eyes, he wanted to taste her sweet lips. The minute she shut up he lowered his head and kissed her without any resistance. The kiss was nice but not enough for him.

The storm was a natural aphrodisiac to Rollin. It had brought her body into his arms and her mouth to meet his. Her lips parted and let his tongue inside, sending a surge of pleasure through his body. She went all soft against him, and he held her tighter.

Her soft body pressed firmly against his awoke a desire that had been raging in him from the first day he laid eyes on her. With his arms still around her he took a step forward until she backed into the counter. The taste of her mouth was driving him crazy. He released her and brought his hands to her face, cupping her cheeks in the palm of his hands. With an urgency he'd never felt before, he unsnapped her raincoat and pushed it off her shoulders and down her back until it hit the floor. Then did the same with his.

He cupped and caressed her breast through her T-shirt until she arched her back and wrapped her arms around his neck. While the lightning and thunder continued all around them, Rollin filled his palms with Tayler's jean-clad bottom and lifted her up until she sat on the counter. In one swift move he pulled her T-shirt from her jeans over her head. Then slid her bra straps off her shoulders, releasing her breasts. She shivered and he lowered his head, taking one soft nipple into his mouth, sucking until it hardened, before moving to the next one. The feel of her erect nipples drove him farther than he intended to go.

With her arms around his neck again, Rollin lifted Tayler from the counter. He unzipped her jeans and smiled as she wiggled to get them over her hips. The minute she did, she kicked them away and reached down to unbuckle his belt. He took his pants down, kicked his way out of his boots and threw everything aside. He couldn't keep his mouth off her body, he realized after pulling her back into his embrace and kissing her everywhere he possibly could. She responded with soft moans and sounds that drove him crazy.

Unable to control his urge any longer, he backed her into the wall. She wrapped her legs around his waist, and her arms around his neck. Thunder drowned out her gasp and moans while Rollin pressed one hand against the wall and kept the other around Tayler's waist.

Then suddenly she threw her head back and uttered, "Rollin, Oh, God! What are we doing?"

Chapter 10

Rollin looked at Tayler, trying to catch his breath.

"Tayler, what's wrong?"

Her head dropped to his neck and her breathing against his skin made his whole body shiver.

"Let's go back in the house. I can't do this out here."

"What? We were close to already doing it."

"Please, Rollin."

He closed his eyes and pulled himself together before slowly letting her down. She quickly gathered her clothes and put them back on. The amount of control he possessed over his body right now surprised even him as he threw his clothes back on as well.

The sky lit up before the mother of all thunderclaps caused Tayler to scream. He pulled her into his arms and kissed her before they made a mad dash for the truck.

Tayler lowered the hood of her jacket and took a

deep breath. In one swift move Rollin turned to her, placed his hand behind her neck and pulled her mouth to his. His tongue found hers warm and soft as he savored her sweetness over and over again.

He devoured every last morsel of her until he couldn't take it any longer. He released her, started the truck and took off through the blinding rain. He kept his eyes on the road, and Tayler kept hers out the window. He would have given anything to read her thoughts.

When they reached the house, Rollin pulled as close as he could to the back door. He turned off the engine and they sprinted toward the house. Like two wet ducks they waddled from the kitchen to the back hallway.

"Stay right there," Rollin said as he hung his slicker on a peg and went to grab a towel from his bathroom. When he returned Tayler had taken off her slicker and stepped out of her sneakers.

He handed her the towel. Still aroused, he needed to touch her, kiss her, or better yet finish what they'd started. She gave her face a couple of soft pats with the towel. They locked eyes and all he could think about was getting her out of her clothes. He took the towel from her and tossed it on the floor. When she looked up, startled, he grabbed her by the waist and pulled her body against his.

He lowered his head and took her bottom lip between his teeth. He bored his hot tongue into her mouth and kissed her so completely this time she came up on her tiptoes and wrapped her arms around his neck. He swept her up in his arms and carried her down the hall to his bedroom. She had no idea how bad he wanted to give his love to her.

* * *

Tayler's heart pounded in her chest and she fought to control the urge to climb all over Rollin. His hands on her behind pressed her into his bulging erection. The throbbing between her legs was unbearable. She needed him the way she needed to breathe.

He stopped outside what she assumed was his bedroom. He put his hand on the door to open it, but stopped.

"Tayler, if I need to stop, you'd better say so now." His voice was deeper than usual.

"Do so and I'll kill you," she whispered.

He grinned and pushed the door open. Tayler's heart beat hard and fast with anticipation as he carried her into the room to his bed.

The minute he lowered her onto the bed he reached down and pulled her T-shirt over her head. He planted sultry kisses from her forehead down the side of her neck. She wanted to rip her clothes off and straddle him until the fire building inside her extinguished. Thunder and lightning continued outside, but it no longer captured Tayler's attention. Her body cried out for Rollin.

As he unfastened his pants, she reached up and pulled his mouth back down to hers. Her kiss was urgent and purposeful. She needed Rollin to feel how bad she wanted him.

He slid his hands behind her back to unclasp her bra. She arched her back as he slid the bra from her shoulders and tossed it with her shirt. She sat up and reached out to touch his muscular chest, feeling the heat against the palm of her hand. Her exposed body shivered as he finished undressing her and then himself. He removed his briefs last, and his package amazed her. He was larger than any man she'd ever been with. She wanted to reach out and touch him, but the opportunity passed. He lowered himself over her and placed his warm mouth over her nipple. She closed her eyes, sucked in a deep breath, and shuddered.

Rollin's arm trembled as he held himself over her. She couldn't help it—she wanted to feel the power. His muscular chest and six-pack abs had already excited her. She reached out and gripped his hairy arms.

Any remaining inhibitions she might have had disappeared as she pushed him off her and onto his back. She straddled him and he cupped her bottom and settled her over him. His body was firm and hard, and she could stare at him all night long. Her pelvic muscles reacted and she couldn't stop herself from grinding against him. She moaned with pleasure as he met her rhythm.

His eyes roamed over her body. "You are the most beautiful, desirable Barbie I've ever seen, and I want you so bad it's blowing my mind."

She bit her bottom lip and grinned down at him. "Then stop teasing me. And please tell me you have a condom?"

Rollin gave Tayler an alluring grin before he sat up and flipped her over onto her back. "Yep." He rolled away from her and over to the side of the bed. Out of the nightstand drawer he produced a gold wrapper. After he rolled back over she helped him place the condom on himself. He spread her legs and slowly eased his love inside her. It took her body more than a minute to adjust to him. He pulled out, giving her a minute to catch her breath, before sliding back inside her, deeper this time. He developed a rhythm, going deeper and deeper each time until her body welcomed him completely. She bit her bottom lip then mouthed, *Thank you.*

Rollin gave her a little pain mixed with a lot of pleasure. He thrust harder and faster now as she wrapped her legs around his thighs and her arms around his neck. If you could combust from pleasure she would have. She threw her head back, closed her eyes, and enjoyed the ride.

He slowed down long enough to cover her mouth with his and kiss her until she thought the room wouldn't stop spinning.

Then he released her mouth and eased out of her.

Tayler loosened her grip around his neck but didn't want to let go. She didn't want it to be over yet, it couldn't be.

"Turn over," he whispered in a sultry voice and helped her flip over.

She rolled over onto her stomach then up on her knees. A second later, his hands gripped her hips and he leaned over to plant succulent kisses along the curve of her back. He massaged her butt before entering her. She took a deep breath when his fingers reached under her and began to stroke her. She opened up like an exotic flower in bloom.

Here she was, lying on this man's bed ass up, and she'd only known him for a week. He made love to her as if he already knew what she liked and how she liked it. He stroked her until she did everything but beg him to stop.

He drove himself into her over and over again, thrusting deeper each time. She pressed her elbows into the pillow and called out his name as she peaked. He filled her with his love and she cried in ecstasy.

Soon after, he collapsed with her onto the bed.

She lay with him pressed against her back trying to catch her breath. Rollin's hot panting breath against Tayler's ear reminded her of where she was. She'd never experienced anything quite like what they'd just done in her entire life. As she came down off her high and her breathing slowed, she snuggled under his arm, cherishing the moment.

After a few minutes, Rollin released her and rolled over onto his back. Tayler rolled over on her back.

"You okay?" he asked in a raspy voice.

She nodded, which was the best she could do at the moment.

What the hell was that! We came together! She'd heard people talk about it, but had never experienced it herself. That was euphoria, a high unlike any drug she could ever imagine. After a deep relaxing breath Tayler stared up at the ceiling.

Rollin lay staring at the ceiling for several minutes also, before he got up. "I'll be right back." He disappeared into the bathroom.

With him gone, her eyes scanned the room for the first time and her good senses returned. She was in Rollin's bedroom, back in his private quarters. An area off-limits to guests. What just transpired was the most spontaneous thing she'd ever done, and with Nicole's cousin! She grabbed the sheet and pulled it up over her naked body. What would she tell Nicole? She had known this would happen if she didn't keep his distance.

"Are you cold?" Rollin asked.

Tayler jumped when she saw him standing butt naked in the doorway. "No."

He started across the room. "Then what are you doing?"

She gripped the cover, holding it close to her breast. "I'm naked."

He stopped and looked down at himself. "No shit, so am I. But you look amazing."

She ran a hand over her face. "Rollin, I don't know what came over me."

He reached for the sheet. "Don't tell me you're about to apologize."

"I don't have anything to apologize for, but, uh…" Tayler tucked the cover around her and wiggled her way to the edge of the bed and stood up.

Rollin looked confused. "Where you goin'?" he asked.

"Where are my clothes?"

He pointed to the pile of clothes on the floor.

She hopped over and snatched up her clothes, then shuffled off to the bathroom. Before closing the door, she glanced back at him standing by the bed with his arms crossed, shaking his head. She then quickly closed the door.

In the bathroom she had a quick mental meltdown. Staring at herself in the mirror, she dropped the cover. Her body still tingled from his touch. She proceeded to put her clothes back on. What had come over her? What was Rollin thinking about the way she had followed him into his bedroom so easily? She sat on the toilet seat, resting her head in the palm of her hands for a few minutes. *What did he just do to me?*

No man had ever made her want to give it up so

easily before. If they had other guests in the house this would never have happened, she told herself. She blamed everything and everyone before admitting to herself nothing happened that she didn't want to happen.

She pulled herself together and opened the bathroom door. She placed Rollin's folded bedspread back on the bed where he sat.

Rollin leaned back on his elbows. "What's wrong? Why did you put your clothes back on?"

"I need to go. I, uh…" she stuttered, unable to get out what she wanted to say. "Thank you."

He looked puzzled. "Thank you?"

"I'm sorry." She made a beeline for the bedroom door and hurried out as fast as she could, leaving Rollin sitting there in his beautiful birthday suit.

Chapter 11

The next morning, Tayler left a note on her door saying she was sleeping in. Rita hadn't returned, and she couldn't face Rollin yet. She rode into town, purchased a local paper, and had breakfast at McDonald's.

Instead of going back to Coleman House she found the visitors' welcome center in town and grabbed some brochures. She decided on a self-guided tour of Danville. She started across the street at Constitution Square, strolling through the old landmarks, and discovering all of Danville's firsts—first college, first post office, first law school—the town was full of history. Then she walked across the street for a cup of coffee before visiting the quaint shops on Main Street. Next stop would be the arts center train exhibit, before she made her way over to the dollhouse museum.

The miniature dollhouses and shops were amazing.

She couldn't believe the amount of detail that went into each structure. The dolls inside, however, actually freaked her out a bit. But even more important was the number of out-of-town dollhouse enthusiasts and history lovers who happened to be visiting. After striking up conversations with several people, she realized these were potential customers for Coleman House.

When Tayler returned to the B and B, several cars were in the parking lot. Maybe more guests had arrived and she wouldn't be there alone with Rollin any longer. The thought made her happy and sad at the same time. She didn't need to be alone with him, but she'd miss the private moments they'd shared.

She got out of the car and strolled inside. As soon as she opened the front door, she heard voices coming from the library. She hadn't seen Rollin's truck outside, so she thought Rita must have been back and was showing the new guests around. But as she passed the library, she glanced in and saw several men inside.

Rollin waved at her, and she waved back but kept walking. She didn't dare go inside to disturb them. Instead, she started up the stairs to her room.

"Have you eaten?"

She stopped at the sound of Rollin's voice and glanced over her shoulder. He'd stepped out of the library. "Yes, I stopped and had a late lunch," she replied.

"Well, if there's anything else you need tonight, don't hesitate to ask. Anything at all," he added with a cocky smile.

A flush of embarrassment crossed her face and she

turned away. "No, I'm fine. Have a good evening." She practically ran up the steps to her room.

Rollin grinned as he turned around to rejoin his business associates in the library. Tayler could run from him now, but sooner or later they'd have to talk about last night. What transpired between them was beautiful and he wanted to tell her how he felt.

"Okay, guys, back to business. I've laid out my finances to you and you know what's on my mind. Now I just need to convince Corra."

Later that evening, Rollin sat on the front porch in one of the rocking chairs watching the sunset. He was enjoying a rare moment when there was nothing that needed his attention. He couldn't get Tayler and last night out of his mind. He could still see her toned, curvy body lying across his bed.

"Excuse me."

Rollin was so deep in thought he hadn't even heard the door open. At the sound of Tayler's voice, he sat up. "Good evening. Come on out."

"I just wanted to thank you for the clean linen and ask for a washcloth."

He sat back and took a deep breath. "Okay, I'll get you one, but come on out here for a minute. I want you to see something."

She glanced back inside before stepping all the way out and releasing the door. "What is it?"

He pointed to the other rocker. "Have a seat."

She let out a heavy sigh then sat down.

Rollin looked across the field at the orange and yellow glow of the setting sun. "Isn't that beautiful?"

Tayler crossed her arms and stared off across the

fields for a few minutes before commenting. "It's amazing. It looks like the sun is about to have a seat in the middle of your field."

"It does, doesn't it? When I was younger, my parents used to sit out here every night until after the sun went down. We had a glider-like seat then. They would be all hugged up, just talking and watching the sunset. Sometimes my mom would fall asleep in my pop's arms. I was too busy catching lightning bugs at the time to appreciate its beauty, but I understood those moments meant something special to them."

"Sunsets are special," she said in a soft low voice.

"When shared with the right person, I believe they are. Otherwise you might not even notice it." He watched her watch the sunset and wished he could hold her in his arms. Special moments like this were meant for special conversations.

"Tayler, I know you don't want to talk about last night, but I wanted to let you know that I'm glad it happened. And I hope it happens again."

She uncrossed her arms as the sun disappeared from sight. "Rollin, we got caught up last night, but you know as well as I do that it never should have happened. If I'm going to stay here the rest of the month, or longer, we need to just forget it ever happened." She stood up.

"Just forget about it, huh?"

She shrugged. "Yes. If you don't mind, I'd like that washcloth now. I need to take a shower."

He stood up. "Yeah, sure, let me get you one." He followed her inside, not believing for a minute that she wanted to forget all about last night. Upstairs in the linen closet, he pulled out a washcloth and met her at the entrance to her room.

"Need anything else?" he asked as he held out the washcloth.

"No, that's it, thanks."

She reached for the washcloth, but he yanked it back. The look she gave him could have been a bullet if she'd had a gun.

He offered the washcloth again and she grabbed it, but he held on.

"Enjoy your day?" he asked.

"Yes, I did. Why?"

He let go of the washcloth. "You wouldn't have been trying to avoid me because of last night, would you?"

She put a hand on her hip. "Don't flatter yourself. I wasn't even thinking about that today. You caught me at a weak moment, that's all."

He chuckled. "Well, the next time I catch you at a weak moment, don't thank me afterward." He backed away from her door.

Her jaw dropped. "I didn't thank you."

"Yes, you did. But that's cool, because here at Coleman House, we aim to please." He gave her a mock salute and headed downstairs. "I'll see you at breakfast in the morning."

"Oh, and there won't be a next time," she assured him before slamming the door.

Chapter 12

Tayler spent the next couple of days being cordial to Rollin and trying not to think about Saturday night. No other guests had checked in, and Rita was still out sick. Tayler did a little antique shopping and took some beautiful landscape pictures with her cell phone. Whenever she saw Rollin, all she could think about was the mind-blowing sex they'd shared.

She'd agreed to meet Corra after her Tuesday evening choir rehearsal to give an empowerment talk to the women of the choir. "Corra, I thought you said there were only ten women in the choir," Tayler said, standing in a room full of beautiful women of all ages and sizes.

"Yeah, about that. I told a few other church members they could come, and you know how news travels in small towns. A few other women invited themselves."

Tayler looked around the room, both surprised and delighted. What she liked most was empowering small groups of women. After a brief introduction from Corra, Tayler stepped up to the podium.

"Ladies, thank you for sticking around tonight. I promise not to take up too much of your time. Corra asked me to speak to you tonight, so I thought I'd start off by telling you who I am, then we'll talk about being at peace with ourselves."

Wednesday morning Tayler decided to go for a walk after breakfast, since the temperature was bearable. She'd reached the garden out back when Rollin strolled up the path to join her. She wanted to turn around and run back inside, but why? She'd have to face him sooner or later.

"Enjoying the gardens?" Rollin asked.

"I am," she responded. "I was going to take a walk," she said, glancing from one path to the other, "but I'm not sure which direction to go."

"That path right there—" he pointed over her left shoulder "—leads down to a nice creek surrounded by wild flowers and a few benches. You might like that," he added.

"That sounds nice and relaxing," she said, looking toward the tree-lined path.

"Just watch out for snakes."

Tayler whipped her head around and caught the grin on his face before he tried to replace it with a more serious look. "You're kidding me, right?"

He shrugged. "You're in the country. Creeks and wooded areas are home to snakes."

"Oh, well, so much for a morning stroll. I don't like snakes." She turned back toward the house.

"Come on." He chuckled and gestured for her to follow him.

She turned slowly but didn't move toward him.

He walked past her. "I'll walk down with you to scare away snakes, and then I promise to leave you alone."

She hesitated for a few seconds before they started down the path together.

"My mom had these paths cleared so she could walk down to the creek and sit and read. She liked to hear the rippling of the water." He looked around at the heavily wooded area on each side of the path.

Tayler felt as if she were walking into the lion's den. Anytime she stood next to Rollin or talked to him, an inability to concentrate on anything other than him took over. He had that kind of effect on her.

"This really is a remarkable place you have here."

He strolled along with his hands clasped behind his back.

"Thank you. My parents loved it—that's why they wanted to share it with so many people. Unfortunately, it's more of a financial drain than anything else these days. Something always needs fixing. Since we have vacancies, I've started minor repairs to all of the rooms upstairs except yours."

"It doesn't have to be a drain, that's for sure. I have a head full of ideas that could help you. Like new branding and more of a social media presence. With the right partnerships you could be at capacity almost every week."

He gave her a knowing smile and nodded. "I see you're amazing in more ways than one."

She let on as though she had no idea what he was talking about. "Excuse me?"

"You're a woman of many talents. I don't doubt that the businesswoman in you wants to pick this place apart."

"You'll have to let me show you what I do. I don't pick businesses apart. I build partnerships that improve business for all parties."

"I bet you do." Rollin stopped as they reached the clearing next to the creek, where two iron benches sat side by side.

Tayler took a seat and listened to the rippling of the water.

"This is where I leave you," Rollin said as he turned around.

Tayler didn't want him to leave, but she couldn't ask him to stay, either. He had work to do.

The next morning Tayler had breakfast with Rollin and Kevin. She even rode out to the field with Kevin to get vegetables for the day's meal. When she returned, Rollin was out working, and Rita was still at home sick, so Tayler found her lemonade pitcher and whipped up a batch herself. She hoped Rollin wouldn't mind her messing around in the kitchen, because she missed Rita's afternoon lemonade.

Soon afterward, Corra showed up and they worked on the fund-raiser in the library.

"Tayler, thank you so much again for Tuesday night. The ladies can't stop talking about you. Everybody wants you to come speak at their school, or book club meeting, or whatever."

"You're welcome. I'm glad they were so responsive."

"Oh, they were motivated, and inspired. My phone hasn't stopped ringing. I have a feeling this is the start of something great."

"I hope so, Corra."

"Oh, by the way, we've got the fund-raiser website fixed. All the problems you pointed out are no longer there."

"That's great. Who fixed it?"

"Chris—he's one of Rollin's partners. He's a computer wizard and I didn't even know it. He's a cutie pie, too."

"Hmm, do I detect a little interest in this guy?"

"Girl, that man is not interested in a woman with two kids, especially not his boy's younger sister. He ran with Rollin in high school and I used to have the biggest crush on him."

"Then why don't you ask him out? You'll never know how he feels about kids if you don't say anything."

Corra shook her head. "Call me old-fashioned, but I don't ask men out. I'm just not that aggressive."

"If you can get half the businesses in this town to give money for a fund-raiser in a recession, you're aggressive enough to ask him out."

Corra blushed. "So you just ask men out when you want to?"

"I have."

"Yeah, but you seem like the type of woman who goes after what she wants. That's just not me. Besides,

I believe a relationship has more of a chance when the man is the one doing the asking."

"What if he's too shy to ask?"

"I've got two kids. I don't need a shy man."

Tayler laughed. "Yeah, but men like the woman to be the aggressor every now and then—that way he knows you want him. Men risk rejection all the time."

"I guess you're right, but…"

Tayler listened to Corra, but her mind drifted off to Saturday night and the way she'd run out on Rollin. The way she'd rejected him after he'd made her feel as if she was on top of the world. She hadn't thought about it from his perspective before now.

Corra and Tayler were deep in conversation when the doorbell rang. Corra answered it and in walked a middle-aged man, a woman and two little boys. They were passing through Danville and wanted to know if there were any vacancies.

"Sure, come on in," Corra said.

Tayler knew the other guest rooms were being repaired.

"Have a seat and I'll get you all checked in." Corra stepped back into the library. "Tayler, I'll be right back."

"Corra, do you have another room ready?" Tayler whispered.

"There should be," Corra said. "We have four rooms upstairs," she added in a whisper.

Tayler shook her head. "Rollin's making repairs in the other three rooms, so none of them are guest ready."

"You're kidding." Corra turned around to see the family had stepped out to get their luggage.

Tayler followed Corra to the front door.

"Shoot, what do I do now? They're bringing their bags in."

Tayler had an idea. "Are the upstairs bedrooms the only ones in the house?"

"No, the family quarters are down here, but they're small. Besides, Rollin would kill me if I put them back there."

"I'll move. We can get my room cleaned up for them. Tell them to go get something to eat and when they return the room will be ready. It has two full-size beds in it—it's perfect."

Corra turned to her. "No, I can't ask you to move."

"You didn't, I volunteered."

Corra grabbed Tayler's shoulders. "You're a god-send, you know that?"

"I'll run and pack." She winked at Corra.

"And I need to find Rollin."

Tayler ran upstairs and threw her clothes back in her suitcase. She never fully unpacked her suitcase regardless of how long she stayed anywhere.

A few minutes later, the bedroom door swung open and Corra walked in. "Okay, we've got an hour before they get back. Wow, you're almost packed already?"

"I never really unpack," Tayler said before going into the bathroom for her toiletries. "What did Rollin say?"

"I haven't found him yet. He's not answering his cell phone, so I just left a message. I'll go grab some stuff and start on the bathroom."

Together they cleaned the bathroom, changed the linen and vacuumed the floor.

Corra stopped working and looked around the

room. "My mother used to love when guests showed up. She lived for this stuff. All she wanted to do was decorate these rooms and cook for people. She was good at it, too."

"That's what Rollin said. Did she do most of the work herself?"

"Yep, whatever she couldn't get me and Rollin to do, anyway. We were little innkeepers in training. She taught us how to properly make a bed, and we baked cookies every day, it seemed like. Most of the time I hated it because I'd rather be out with my girlfriends."

"And she still doesn't like it," a deep voice interjected.

Corra and Tayler turned toward the sound of Rollin's voice. He took up the entire entrance and looked mad as hell.

"I got your message. What the hell are you doing, Corra?"

"I knew you'd be a little testy, but Tayler and I have everything under control."

Rollin turned his enraged look toward Tayler. "You're a guest. You don't have to move out of this room. I'd like to have a word with my sister."

"Rollin, it was my idea," Tayler offered.

He looked taken aback. "What do you mean, it was your idea?"

"I remembered you saying the other rooms were being repaired, so I suggested my room. I don't mind moving at all."

He crossed his arms and tilted his head toward Corra. "And where is she moving to?"

"The second bedroom downstairs, where else? And you need to get these rooms up here completed. Rollin, I know what you're trying to do, and you are not closing this B and B. If I have to quit my job and come work here myself, we're not closing."

Tayler detected the pissed look on Rollin's face and decided it was time to leave. "I'll step out and let you guys talk," she said and backed out into the hallway. She eased on down the steps and into the foyer, holding her bag of toiletries. She hadn't expected such an eventful vacation. One thing was for sure, she'd have a story to tell when she returned home.

A few minutes later, the door upstairs swung open and Rollin came down the steps with her suitcase and laptop case in hand. "Follow me. I'll show you to your room."

He proceeded down the hall toward his bedroom, which gave Tayler a flashback of their night together. They walked past his room to the next door. He held it open for her to enter.

"This is the family guest room. I'm sorry that it's not as brightly decorated as the one upstairs."

She looked around at the room decorated in warm gold and burgundy colors with a four-poster mahogany bed. It had everything the other room had, except a desk for her to work on.

"Where's the bathroom?" she asked.

"Through here." He walked over and opened the door to the bathroom. "It's an adjoining bathroom."

She looked up at him.

"Yeah, that means we'll have to share. I wish Corra had told you that before you volunteered to give up your room."

"That's okay, we'll make it work. This is turning out to be more of an adventure than a mere vacation."

He walked back into the bedroom and to the door. "I'll let you get your stuff all settled, then."

"Rollin, one of the reasons I volunteered to move is that I agree with Corra—you shouldn't close the B and B. The growth potential is phenomenal. And with Rita being out, I thought I could help out a little bit. It'll give me an opportunity to test out some of the ideas I spoke to you about yesterday."

He arched a brow, then let out a deep sigh. "We can discuss your ideas, but don't worry about helping out. Corra's gonna do that, since her mouth got you into this."

She glanced down for a moment. "Ah, can we tackle the elephant in the room before this goes any farther?"

He crossed his arm and gave her a slow, appraising glance. "And what would that be?"

"I don't want you to think I'm down here because of what happened Saturday night. I'm not trying to send mixed signals or anything."

He widened his stance and tilted his head. "Okay."

"I don't want you to think I jump in bed with just anybody, because I don't."

He shook his head. "I don't make assumptions about you anymore, remember. Not that I consider myself *just* anybody, anyway."

"Well, that was the first time I've ever done anything that spontaneous and reckless. You don't have to worry about that happening again."

He nodded. "Let me see if I've got this right. You don't want me to think you orchestrated this whole thing just so you could get closer to me in hopes of me making love to you again, is that right?"

She slowly nodded her head. "Yes. That's the elephant I was referring to."

He chuckled and shook his head. "Thank you for clearing that up. For a minute there I thought the other night might have meant something to you, but I see I was wrong." He turned around and walked out.

Tayler opened her mouth to say something, but changed her mind. Whatever she'd say, he'd find a way to twist her words around. Saturday night meant more to her than he knew, but she couldn't let him know that.

Chapter 13

That night Tayler climbed into bed knowing Rollin was on the other side of the bathroom door. She rolled over and pulled the cover close to her body. She could still picture him kissing his way down to her breasts and could feel the heat building inside her. Why had she let it go that far? Did she need a man that bad?

The other side of the bathroom door opened and she turned back over. She could see a light at the foot of the door frame. Rollin was in the bathroom. She wrapped her hands around her pillow and stared at the light thinking about the way he'd kissed her while holding her face in the palms of his hands.

The shower came on and she squeezed her legs together. He'd taken his clothes off. After days of speculating what he was like in bed, she'd found out. The only problem was, now she couldn't get him out of her mind.

As good as the sex was, Tayler knew it could never happen again. They had merely filled a need for each other. She hadn't been with a man in quite a while, and he possibly hadn't had a woman in a while. She rationalized the whole situation until she made herself feel better. Now she had to make sure Nicole never found out or she'd never hear the end of it.

Rollin stood under the showerhead and let the water cool him off. Tayler's presence on the other side of the bathroom door made sleep almost impossible. He turned his face up into the water and tried to let it wash all thoughts of her out of his mind. He grabbed a washcloth and bar of soap. The more he thought about her, the harder he scrubbed.

He could still see her lying on his bed, legs spread, displaying her love, and he wanted her. Being near her and smelling her perfume caused his body to react in ways he didn't want it to. He squeezed himself, thinking about how bad he wanted her. He wanted her tonight, tomorrow night and every night until her departure.

He quickly finished his shower and stepped out. After air-drying he pulled on his pajama pants and found himself at the door leading to Tayler. He wondered what she would do if he went into her room tonight. Would she let him make love to her this time until she screamed his name? He reached out and grabbed the knob.

Tayler bit her bottom lip as she stared at the shadow at the foot of the door and saw the knob move. Rollin was out of the shower and coming to her. Her brain said, *no!* Her body screamed, *yes!* She needed—no, she yearned for—complete, uninhibited sex with this man who penetrated her every fantasy.

Too soon the shadow moved away and the bathroom light went out. She rolled over, grabbed the extra pillow, and shoved it between her knees.

When Tayler woke the next morning, Rollin had already used the bathroom and left. She showered and dressed, eager to meet the Evans family and test some of her ideas for the B and B. Most of all, she was glad to have other people in the house.

After they were informed Rita had the flu, Corra returned with her kids and played host the entire weekend. Tayler persuaded Corra to let her help with the meals and a few other chores. They took care of the house, while Rollin spent most of his time on the farm. It was all exactly the type of diversion Tayler had hoped for.

Tayler made Rita's lemonade every afternoon, while Corra baked the cookies. Although Rollin reminded her on several occasions that she didn't have to do anything, she wanted to.

Corra's children played with the twins, and when the Evanses weren't in town, they roamed through the gardens or lay in the hammocks out back. The whole family joined Tayler and Kevin for morning truck rides to pick vegetables, and they loved it.

Tayler couldn't believe how much she enjoyed playing innkeeper. There were no presentations to prepare, no metrics to adhere to and, best of all, no long boring meetings to attend. Once when Corra left to take care of fund-raiser business, Tayler pretended the B and B was hers. She was having the time of her life.

Every night Tayler heard Rollin in the bathroom and watched the light underneath the door until it went out. Instead of memories of their night together fading, they strengthened. She crossed his path in the hallway several times and tried her best not to touch him. The smell of him was orgasmic. His touch sent her body into a quivering state. Thank goodness the guests had shown up when they did.

When Monday afternoon arrived she hated to see the Evans family leave. Corra went home, and Tayler was alone with Rollin again.

Later that evening, she stood in the bathroom mirror taking off her makeup when the door opened and Rollin walked in. He stopped short once he saw her.

"I'm sorry, I didn't know you were in here." He backed up.

"That's okay. I'm finished." She zipped up her makeup pouch. "You can come on in." She tossed her tissue in the wastebasket and moved away from the sink.

"You know, you really don't need to wear makeup," he said.

"Oh, I need it, all right. I feel naked without any on."

He stepped over to the sink to wash his hands. "Millions of women wish they looked as good as you do without makeup."

"Thank you," she said as she reached for the door to her room. Then she turned around, "Rollin, Corra and I made some small purchases for the B and B this weekend, but I'd like to go over some of my more expensive ideas with you. I can show you on my computer when you have time."

He reached for a hand towel and dried his hands. "Seeing as how you two are ganging up on me, sure, why not. How about after dinner tonight?"

She smiled. "Great." She went back into her room and closed the door. A shiver ran down her spine as she realized they would be having dinner alone again tonight.

For dinner Tayler changed into a simple white summer dress and flat silver sandals. The minute she left her room, she could smell onions sautéing.

When she entered the dining room, the low light and soft music from the stereo in the library had created a romantic ambience. The door that led to the kitchen was propped open. She walked through.

"Is there anything I can help you with?" she asked.

He turned around and stared at her for a few seconds before shaking his head. "I've got it. Help yourself to a glass of wine, though."

She stepped over to the counter, where an opened bottle of red wine and two empty glasses sat. She remembered what happened the last time she drank his wine, so she poured herself a small glass. "What are you preparing?"

"Lamb, with some couscous and vegetables."

"It smells wonderful."

He joined her and poured himself a glass of wine. "You smell wonderful, too," he said.

"Thank you." Tayler didn't want the evening to get off on the wrong foot, so she avoided eye contact with him at all costs. Every time he looked into her eyes it weakened her determination not to have sex with him again.

"Since you have everything in here under control, I'll just grab my computer for after dinner."

"Sure," he said and returned to the stove.

She left the kitchen and returned seconds later with her laptop. While Rollin finished dinner, she sipped her wine and glanced at a few work emails but didn't feel the need to respond to anything. She was enjoying her vacation. Minutes later, Rollin emerged from the kitchen with platters of food.

After dinner and some small talk, Tayler opened her laptop again. "You know I've only been here two weeks, but I see room for improvement."

"It's only been two weeks?"

She nodded. "Yes."

"Wow. It seems like you've been here longer than that."

"Yeah, it does. So don't take my suggestions the wrong way. Part of my job is working on process improvements. So, I'm always trying to figure out how to do things better and more efficiently."

"Let's get to it, then." He moved from his side of the table to the seat next to her.

Tayler could smell the spicy scent of his cologne and feel the heat from his body and almost lost her train of thought. In response, her body tensed up.

"First, I think you need a new website. Something that will take you into the future. You can offer discounts in connection with some local events, festivals or family reunions."

He nodded. "I agree with you."

"I don't see any business cards. They're inexpensive and—"

"I have some."

"Okay, then you need to set them out—that way your guests can take them home and pass them out to family and friends. And businesses that you partner with should have them on display, as well. I don't remember seeing any around town since I've been here."

"I've been too busy to follow up on that."

"Okay, well, that's simple to fix." She had more ideas, but with him so close she found it difficult to concentrate.

"Is that it?" he asked, looking at her computer screen.

"No, let's see." She glanced at the screen but could feel his eyes on her. The sensual music didn't make the situation any easier. She tried to ignore it and tapped on her computer screen.

"We purchased a coffeemaker and a few other very inexpensive fixes. Also, in regard to repairs… Yeah, uh, you might want to hire a handyman, or keep one on a short leash. Your rooms should be available and preferably booked at all times."

He leaned back in his seat. "I agree with you again."

"And I think you need some help other than Rita and Wallace."

He shook his head. "Can't afford it. Corra steps in when I need her."

"And she does a great job. I noticed that this week. But what if she hadn't been available? Say one of the kids got sick or something—what would you have done?"

"I would have handled everything myself."

"Rollin, you're a one-man band here. What would happen if you got sick?"

He sat up and stretched his arms over his head. "I don't get sick."

She laughed. "How come men always say that? You can get sick like anybody else."

"I didn't say I couldn't get sick. I said I don't get sick. I can't remember the last time I was sick, with anything."

"Well, you need to be prepared for anything."

"I try to be."

Again she sensed his eyes moving down her body and momentarily lost her train of thought. "Okay, so you can't hire someone. Let's see what I have next."

He leaned closer and draped an arm over the back of her chair. The temperature in the room climbed faster than a rocket headed for outer space. She looked at him, her face inches from his lips, and leaned back.

"You need a bigger monitor," he said. "What is that, fifteen inches?"

"Fifteen and a half," she replied, and turned her gaze back to the screen." She dabbed at the sweat above her lip, hoping he wouldn't notice she was on fire.

"I'm not too close for you, am I?" he asked in a husky voice.

She turned her laptop toward him. "Here, does that help?" she asked, barely able to breathe. The top two buttons of his shirt lay open and she caught a glimpse of his chest. His reaction to her kisses against his chest the other night resurfaced and she bit her bottom lip.

"I had a newsletter but couldn't keep it up."

"Huh?"

"The next thing on your list." He pointed to the monitor. "A newsletter. When I took over I created a monthly newsletter, but with all the farmwork, I couldn't keep it up."

"Oh, yeah, uh, there are companies that will do that for you. All you have to do is sign up. That's simple and inexpensive. I can have that done in no time."

He smiled down at Tayler. "You've done enough for me. I can't ask you to do that." He stood up and gathered their plates.

"Actually, I've already looked into it."

"You're on top of everything, aren't you?" he asked as he stepped around the table.

Tayler took a deep breath after a flashback of her straddling him on his bed made her blush. She was indeed on top of things. "I try to be," she responded with a smile.

"Would you like another glass of wine?"

"No, thank you, I'm good. But I'm going to have to get some of that to take home with me. It's a local winery, right?"

"Yeah, I'll get you some," he responded from inside the kitchen.

Once he left the room, she took her foot and pushed his chair over. After she finished her wine she would excuse herself for the night. Rollin's presence was intoxicating enough without the aid of alcohol.

"Sounds like you and Corra conspired over the weekend to turn this place around." He sat down and leaned back in his chair. "Or put me in the poorhouse."

"I think you can turn it around. You won't make hotel money, but I believe you can be profitable."

He scratched his head and laughed. "I can't believe I'm having this conversation with a guest."

"Don't think of me as a guest. Think of me as a friend of the family."

He set his glass down and wiped the sides of his mouth before glancing over at her. "Truthfully, I stopped thinking of you as a guest a few nights ago."

Tayler took a deep breath and stared down into her empty wineglass. *You need to get up now and go to bed.* The music had stopped.

"I want you to be more than a guest to me."

She didn't have a reply for that, because for one night she'd enjoyed the hell out of being more to him. She looked up from her glass. Rollin leaned forward and rested his forehead in his hand, as if he were struggling with something. Maybe he was regretting what he'd said.

Tayler couldn't stand the uncomfortable silence and stood up after a bit. "Do you mind if I put some music back on?" she asked as she walked into the library.

"Help yourself."

"What do you like?" she asked.

"Anything old-school," he said, getting up and joining her in the library. "I like R. Kelly, Musiq, Anthony Hamilton, Mariah Carey, Prince—you name it."

She scanned through the huge music collection. "How about Sade? I don't know a man that doesn't like her."

He nodded. "I've definitely got a soft spot for Sade. I just like good R&B music."

He stood alongside her and reached out for a selection. "How about this one?" he asked before turning on the music.

Tayler listened as the sensual voice of Maxwell emerged from the speakers. Lovemaking music. Fearing what was to come, she turned away from him. Her heart beat in double time. *Lord, don't let this man touch me.*

Chapter 14

He reached for her hand. "Tayler, where you goin'?"

She turned back around and looked up into his eyes. His gaze was on her mouth and she shivered with anticipation. She struggled with herself to resist him, but his love was so good, she was in a losing battle.

His hands slid down her arms and he laced his fingers between hers. "I can't keep my hands off you," he said, his voice close to a whisper.

She looked down at their intertwined fingers and watched him raise her hand to his mouth and kiss it. Her stomach fluttered. He stepped closer and kissed her forehead. Tayler placed her head against his firm, hard chest as he wrapped his arms around her. *I'm so weak for this man.* She begged for strength.

"Rollin, we can't do this again."

"Can't do what? We can't dance?" he asked in a soft,

controlled voice. His body swayed with the music and she found herself following his lead. His leg shifted, his thigh pressed between her legs and her leg followed. They slow danced in the middle of the library.

He ignited a fire inside Tayler that intensified when he reached down and placed his hand under her chin, bringing her face up to meet his. He kissed her lips ever so gently and Tayler closed her eyes. Her head told her to pull away from his embrace before it was too late, but her body had a mind of its own and wanted nothing more than to revel in his embrace.

His lips left hers and she moaned.

"I want to make love to you," he whispered in her ear. "I've tried to fight it, but I can't. I need you tonight."

Tayler felt her stomach clench as she looked up into his smoldering eyes. If he only knew the things she wanted to do to him, but dared not express, he'd be overjoyed. At that moment, her brain lost the battle and her body took over.

She reached up and held his face between her hands and kissed him with an intensity she hadn't even known she possessed. She was like a wild woman starving to taste his lips again. He moaned into her mouth and held her so tight he lifted her from the floor and walked over to the couch, where he placed her on her back.

He wasted no time covering her exposed neck and shoulders with kisses. His warm breath against her skin and in her ear excited her to the point of dizziness. He braced himself with one hand and raised her dress with the other. He kissed her from her navel to her breasts, and then sat up, pulling her with him.

Tayler helped him pull her dress up and over her head, and then lay back down, gazing up at him. He traced a finger along the edge of her bra before popping the front snap. She took a deep breath and reached out for his belt. An uncontrollable blaze burned inside her.

Rollin placed his hand over hers. "Slow down, baby," he said with a chuckle. "We've got all night."

He reached down with both hands and massaged her breasts. "Besides, I want to make sure you can't call tonight a reckless act." He bent over and took turns feasting on one nipple then the other. He raised his head and gazed down into her eyes with a look that said he was as aroused as she was. His breathing was quick, and his skin was hot to the touch.

She was so drunk with desire she heard herself moan.

The throbbing between her legs was intense. Her body trembled on the verge of an explosion. She turned her head and gritted her teeth to keep from screaming.

He sat up again and she reached for his belt. This time he let her unbuckle his belt and unzip his pants. He watched her with heavy eyelids. When she finished, he stood up and took his jeans off. He took her by the hips and slid her panties off.

She yearned so badly to have him extinguish the fire burning inside her, she arched her body up to him. He positioned himself back over her and caressed the inside of her thighs until her legs slowly opened, and then he entered her with two fingers. She squirmed around underneath him before he ventured deeper inside her. His thumb found its own pleasurable spot and Tayler nearly lost her mind.

Her body shuddered and her breathing came in short little pants. He stroked and massaged her, driving her over the edge. She loved every minute of it and thrust her pelvis up in response to his touch.

"This is for you, baby," Rollin whispered in her ear. "You're so beautiful. I want to watch you come."

Her head tossed and turned and her body bucked so hard she thought she'd fall off the couch. He had her heart pounding in her chest and her legs trembling as he worked magic with his fingers. He pulled his fingers out of her and concentrated on the tiny bud that begged for all the attention. His touch was light as a feather but still managed to push all her buttons. Tayler threw her hands over her head and clutched the arm of the couch. Her body throbbed and she cried out from sheer delight. She shuddered from such an intense orgasm and gasped for air.

"Oh, God!" She squeezed her legs together, unable to take it any longer.

As aftershocks riddled her body, Rollin lowered his mouth to hers and gave her a deep, intoxicating kiss. She lay there naked and sated with closed eyes as she regained her breathing.

He held her and whispered into her ear. "Now, that was no reckless act, agreed?"

She opened her eyes, kissed him on the neck and then exhaled a deep gratifying sigh. "Agreed."

Minutes later, Tayler followed Rollin down the hall to his bedroom, where they spent the rest of the night in orgasmic heaven.

The next day after breakfast Rollin worked around the farm while Tayler tried to relax on the front porch and read. It wasn't working, so she pulled out her cell phone and took a few pictures of the house and then drafted the first Coleman House newsletter.

Rollin came back to the house that afternoon dusty and dirty, but to Tayler, he looked sexier than ever.

"Let me shower and change right quick, then you can ride into town with me," Rollin said after he greeted Tayler with a kiss.

"Um." She licked her lips.

He laughed. "What have you been doing all morning?"

"Working on the Coleman House newsletter. I've sketched out a first draft that I'll show you later. And a ride into town would be perfect. I saw a fountain in the town square that would look perfect in the newsletter."

His brows creased. "Who has time to update a monthly newsletter?"

"Relax, it doesn't have to go out monthly. Once I set it up it'll be a breeze to maintain. Either you or Corra can send it out at an agreed-upon time frame."

He opened the front door and she followed him inside. "So this is how it starts, huh? Women start making little changes and the next thing you know they're running the joint."

"Lucky for you I'm only here for a few months. Otherwise, yes, I would take over." She reached out and swatted him on the butt.

"Aren't I lucky," he said before walking down the hall to his room.

Tayler carried her laptop inside, changed and waited for Rollin on the front porch.

The drive into town was Norman Rockwell all over again. Small-town folk going about their business in the normal way. No taxis zipping in and out of traffic. No trains screeching overhead. As a matter of fact, she didn't even hear one horn blow. Maybe she was delusional, but she felt a peace come over her body that she'd never felt before.

Rollin let Tayler out on Main Street to browse through the many quaint shops while he went to take care of some business. They'd agreed to meet up at a restaurant called Cue on Main Street. After sampling several shops, it didn't take Tayler long to find Cue. Rollin was already waiting inside.

He stood up and pulled out her chair as she approached. "What did you buy?" he asked, pointing to the bag in her hand as she sat down.

She reached inside and whipped out her treat on a stick. "A caramel apple, can you believe it? I haven't had one of these in years. I stopped at this cute little shop that had an assortment of a little of everything inside."

Rollin smiled. "You're really enjoying yourself, aren't you?"

She smiled in return. "Yes, I am. Far more than I thought I would. I love this little town. I spoke to the woman in the shop about partnering with Coleman House, and she seemed pretty excited about it."

"You what?"

Tayler sighed. "Rollin, I really think you need to add a small gift shop at the house. Or at least sell some local things on consignment. It'll add a little flavor to the B and B and won't cost you anything."

"So where do we put these little gifts?" he asked.

She shrugged. "Don't worry, I'll think of something."

They ordered lunch and continued to discuss Tayler's ideas until Rollin changed the subject and Tayler's mood.

"So what was growing up like for Tayler? You hardly ever talk about home."

She looked around. "It wasn't like this, that's for sure. I grew up in Rockford, Illinois. In a tiny two-bedroom apartment. My mother worked two jobs to support me, my sister and my brother. My father left when I was young. I saw him once after I graduated from high school, but that was it."

"Wow, I'm sorry to hear that. I hate to hear about any man skipping out on his family."

"Yeah, well, we got over it. Everyone survived and went their separate ways."

"Where's your family now?"

"My mom and sister are still in Rockford. My brother joined the service and he's stationed in Germany. I went to school in Chicago and never looked back. It wasn't very far away, but it seemed like worlds away."

"How often do you get back home?"

She lowered her head, wishing he hadn't asked her that. "Not very often. I've been pretty busy with work and squeezing in speaking engagements when I can."

He didn't say anything, only nodded.

Tayler took a deep breath. "My family wasn't like yours. We've never been particularly close."

"You've done very well for yourself under the circumstances. A VP position with any company is a huge accomplishment. You should be proud of yourself."

She didn't usually discuss her family dynamics with

anyone. But Rollin had opened her up so much in the last couple of weeks she found it easy to talk to him.

"I am proud of myself."

"You're a very special woman, you know that?"

She leaned into the table and smiled. "How special am I?"

"Why don't we head back to the house, and I'll show you."

He winked at Tayler, and she shuddered.

Chapter 15

If Rita hadn't returned Friday morning, Tayler would have stayed right where she had been for the last couple of nights—in Rollin's bed. However, her arrival had sent Tayler scrambling back to her room. Somehow she'd have to explain why she hadn't moved back upstairs since the guests had left.

After dodging Rita's probing eyes, Rollin treated Tayler to a new experience in the middle of a strawberry patch.

"Here, taste this." He fed her a plump, juicy strawberry.

She hesitated and then glanced up at him before taking a bite. The berry exploded in her mouth, sending sweet juice everywhere. Some slid down the side of her mouth and she reached to wipe it up, but Rollin beat her to it.

With his tongue, he caught the running juices and licked his way to her mouth. Once there, he played a game of hide-and-seek, his tongue darting in and out of her mouth before sticking around to taste the sweet juices.

"Um, that was good," he said after kissing her.

Tayler did a 360 to see if anybody saw what had just took place. A few workers were at the other end of the patches but hadn't noticed them.

"Want another one?" Rollin offered.

"Are those things clean?" she asked, wrinkling her nose.

"If this wasn't an organic farm, I'd say no. Since it is, I've wiped it off on my shirt." He offered her another one.

She opened her mouth and closed her eyes while he fed her. "Somehow that doesn't make it any cleaner to me. I'm gonna tell Rita you're eating all the strawberries instead of picking them," she said.

Rollin picked up the small bucket and handed it to her. "I'm just thankful she's back. I don't want to make her mad by returning empty-handed, so let's get to picking."

"I can't wait until she fixes the pie. I've never had a strawberry pie from scratch before." Tayler stooped down next to the bush and Rollin joined her.

"You've lived a pretty sheltered life, haven't you, girl?"

"No way. I've traveled everywhere and have done a little bit of everything." She picked one strawberry and put it into the bucket. The next one she wiped off and ate.

"Yeah, but until you came here you'd never picked

your own food, eaten any organic foods, drunk herbal tea or experienced an orgasm that had you speaking in tongues."

She stopped and stood up. "What?"

"You know, last night, when you screamed my name and something that sounded like you were speaking another language."

"Oh, please, stop flattering yourself." She rolled her eyes and continued picking berries.

"So, you didn't scream my name?"

She shrugged. "Maybe once or twice, but—"

"But nothing," he cut her off. He reached over and dropped a handful of strawberries in her bucket. "This last week has been a new experience for you. I know, baby, just call me your professor."

She laughed. Tayler hated to admit it, but after the exquisite orgasm he gave her on the couch, he was her teacher.

She held a strawberry toward the sky. "Okay, I was not speaking in tongues, more like gibberish or something," she said with a laugh.

He walked over and dropped another handful of strawberries in her bucket. "Whatever it was, I loved it," he said between clenched teeth and then took her face in his hands and bent down for a kiss. "We need to repeat it tonight."

His kisses were irresistible to her now. They stood there kissing like two high school sweethearts until she reluctantly pulled away from his spellbinding lips.

"Stop, we have to get back to the house."

"I know. Rita's waiting and I've got some 'splaining to do."

"Okay, let's head back."

They walked back to the truck, where Rollin dumped the berries into a waiting cooler. During the short ride back he entertained Tayler with one joke after another. When the house came into view, Tayler saw a small car parked next to hers.

"Looks like you have guests," Rollin said.

Rollin dropped Tayler off at the front door while he drove his truck around back. Tayler opened the front door and heard a familiar laugh. She stopped dead in her tracks. She backed out onto the porch and closed the door.

Shit, what is she doing here? Tayler paced around the porch for several seconds in order to pull herself together. Rollin had driven around back to empty the truck bed. She needed to talk to him before he came in, but it was too late. She took a deep breath and entered the house.

Inside the library, Rita and Nicole sat chatting it up.

"Surprise! There's my girl." Nicole jumped up from the couch when she saw Tayler. She threw her arms up and met Tayler in the doorway, giving her a big hug.

Tayler's posture stiffened as she hugged her back. "What are you doing here?" she asked, her voice rising in pitch.

"I flew in for my mom's birthday." Nicole placed her hands on her hips and gave Tayler a thumbs-up. "Well, don't you look like a new woman, good and rested. Country life suits you, huh?"

"It does. I love it," Tayler answered with a big smile.

Rita cleared her throat. "I'll let you girls talk." She eased out of the library.

Tayler tried unsuccessfully to make eye contact with Rita. She didn't know if Rita knew she'd been sleeping in Rollin's room, but the last thing she wanted was for Nicole to find out.

"That's great. Didn't I tell you you'd like it here?"

"You were right." Tayler walked into the library and sat on the couch. Nicole joined her and she smiled up at her friend, thinking about the good times she and Rollin had had the last couple of nights.

"Rita said Rollin's really been showing you around the farm."

Tayler's voice cracked. "Yes, he has. The house, the barn—I even went to the market with them once."

Nicole playfully reached out and whacked Tayler on the arm. "So, how you feelin', chick? Are you all rested and ready to get back to work?"

Tayler laughed. "I'm rested and reenergized, that's for sure. But I've only been here three weeks—the vacation's not over yet." She wasn't ready to discuss work. All she wanted to do was crawl back in bed with Rollin.

"There's my long-lost cousin." Rollin came through the door with a big smile on his face.

"Hey, cuz." Nicole jumped up and ran over to throw her arms around him.

"What's been up, girl?"

Nicole stepped back and gave him an admiring glance. "Man, you're lookin' good. Farmwork definitely agrees with you." She squeezed his arm. "Look at those guns."

He flexed his arm. "Yeah, it's a real workout." Then he stepped back. "But look at you. You've lost weight and everything."

She sashayed around in a circle. "I lost a few

pounds, but you know, a sister always has looked good."

Tayler laughed and shook her head. That was Nicole, always complimenting herself in the third person.

Rollin laughed as well. "You haven't changed one bit."

"Nope, and I don't plan to, either. Thanks for taking such good care of my girl here."

Rollin glanced over at Tayler and grinned. "It's been a pleasure."

Tayler crossed her legs and lowered her gaze to keep from blushing.

"Don't tell me you came all the way down here to check up on her," Rollin asked.

"No, it's Mama's birthday. I flew in to surprise her. Then I had to ride over and see how my girl's doing, especially after the frantic phone calls I received when she arrived."

"Oh, yeah?" Rollin arched one curious brow. "What did she say?"

"That was weeks ago," Tayler protested.

Nicole went on. "She did everything but curse me out."

"Nicole, you don't need to tell him—" Tayler held out her hand, trying to shut her up.

"Especially after she became the only guest, she freaked out. Man, she did not want to stay here alone with you." Nicole was the only one in the room who laughed at that.

Rollin stood there with his arms crossed and his stance wide, grinning at Tayler.

Oh, how she needed Nicole to shut up or change the subject. Then she realized their body language must have given something away, because Nicole shot a glance at Rollin first, then her. "So, what have you done to my friend here, because she hasn't called in over a week."

He shrugged. "Why don't you ask her?"

Nicole's eyes widened and Tayler came to her feet. "He's taught me about organic farming. I'm learning to appreciate what I eat, for one. This place is a real education."

Nicole sucked at her teeth and nodded. "Mm-hmm."

Tayler knew Nicole too well. She wasn't buying it.

"Well, I need to clean up. I'll let you ladies talk. Nicole, you're sticking around for a while, aren't you?" Rollin asked.

"Not taking off till me and my girl here have a little chat."

He left the room and Tayler eased back down on the couch. Nicole stood over her with her arms crossed.

"You know I didn't buy that educational BS, don't you?"

Tayler shrugged. "I can't tell you what to believe, but this place is a real find."

Nicole flopped down next to her. "Damn, I know he's my cousin, but Rollin is looking fine as hell. I don't remember him having all those muscles. Anything happen between you two?"

Tayler shook her head and tried to look casual.

"You lying hussy."

Tayler held a hand to her chest. "What? You think I would get involved with your cousin?"

"Why not? He's not my man or anything. Hell, if he wasn't family I'd go a round in the sheets with him myself."

Tayler laughed. "You are notoriously horny, aren't you?"

"Girl, you know me, so don't lie." Nicole jumped up again and dashed over to the doorway and peeked out. Then she returned to the couch. "Tayler, it's me, Nicole. The friend you tell everything, remember? Like how your ex had such a small—"

"Nicole!"

"I was going to say a small appetite for—you know," Nicole continued with a laugh.

Tayler crossed her arms and nodded. "You don't have to remind me."

Nicole stretched her arm along the back of the couch. "Come on, Tayler, I want the truth."

"Girl, you can't handle the truth," Tayler teased.

"Ew, no, you didn't!"

"Ladies, help yourselves to some fresh lemonade," Rita called out from the dining room.

Tayler and Nicole left the library for the dining room.

"That's what I'm talking about," Nicole said. "Miss Rita, summer just isn't summer without your lemonade."

"Yeah, Rita, I tried to duplicate your recipe when you were sick, but I didn't do you justice," Tayler admitted.

"Well, thank you, ladies. It's actually pretty easy. I'll write down the recipe for the both of you. Nicole, are you staying for dinner?"

"I would love to, but we're taking Mama over to Springfield to that new steak house for her birthday."

"Oh, I heard that's nice," Rita said.

"So have I," Nicole added.

Tayler poured herself a tall glass of lemonade.

"Who ran things while you were sick?" Nicole asked Rita.

"You know Corra steps in when she has to." Rita glanced over at Tayler. "But Rollin did a good job of handling things, too, didn't he, Tayler?"

Tayler caught the twinkle in Rita's eyes and was sure she knew exactly what had transpired between her and Rollin while she was sick. "Yes, he did." She turned away from them and took a big sip of lemonade.

Rita went back into the kitchen and Nicole cleared her throat. Tayler sensed her start to stay something.

"Drop it," Tayler said, pointing to Nicole.

Nicole held a hand up. "Okay, dropped."

Tayler turned and walked out of the dining room. "Let's get some air."

Nicole followed Tayler out to the front porch and then proceeded to fill her in on everything going on at work since she'd left.

"Which brings me to another reason I drove out here today. Do you remember that women's group I started working with last year, Ladies of Distinction?"

"I think so. Several local news anchors are members?"

"Yes, that's the group. Well, they're planning an empowerment conference next year. And they want the Color of Success to host. With the new director of strategic alliance at MesaCom as the keynote speaker."

Tayler furrowed her brows in confusion.

"Girl, that's you. You know Dustin all but promised you that promotion when you get back. You'll be the first black female director for the company. I think that probably excites Dustin more than you."

Tayler's boss had encouraged her to go for the position as soon as the present director informed him of his plans to leave. The search for a new director had begun, only the results hadn't been announced.

"Nicole, what if I don't get the position?" She'd never doubted herself until today.

"Are you kidding me? You're Dustin's girl. That man loves your ass, and if he wasn't married he'd be all over you and you know it. He agrees with everything you say and do. Who else gets to take two months off, no questions asked?"

"He gave me the time because he feared I'd have a nervous breakdown, not because he likes me."

"Whatever. I still say you're a shoo-in for the position. How about it, though? We can even enlist some of our girls as volunteers. They also want the Color of Success to lead a session."

The front door opened and Rollin strolled out.

Chapter 16

A smile spread across Tayler's face. Rollin's mere presence excited her. Everything about him made her want to be with him, under him and in his arms.

"Tayler," Nicole called out.

Tayler turned back to Nicole. She didn't remember what they were talking about. "What?"

Nicole laughed. "The conference."

"Oh, ah, let me think about it. When will you start working on it?"

"I've already started. That's why I need you back in Chicago now so you can help me."

Rollin had started down the steps, but stopped. He looked at Tayler and she saw a flash of concern cross his face.

"Nicole, I need a few days to think about it."

"Come on, Tayler. This is an opportunity for our

organization to get more exposure, which translates to more sponsorships."

"What conference is that?" Rollin asked.

"I'm trying to get my girl here to come back to Chicago and help me with a woman's empowerment conference. We've run a lot of small community workshops all over the Unites States, but this organization can take us to the next level. I'm talking international."

She turned to Tayler. "Who can talk to these young girls and help steer them in the right direction better than you? Tayler, I know how passionate you are about things like this. I just think…"

Nicole kept yapping but Tayler was checking out Rollin's facial expression to see if he seemed to care if she left or not. If she stayed the full two months, she'd still have several weeks before she had to leave. But was she ready to leave him?

"I don't see why this can't wait another month or so," Tayler said once Nicole finished.

"Sounds like she needs you," Rollin added.

Tayler and Rollin locked eyes. His face was expressionless. Did he even care?

"Yes, I need you," Nicole pleaded. "Besides, you look so relaxed now—what will a few more weeks do?"

Tayler had submerged herself into this slow-paced life and wasn't ready to get back to the rat race. She turned to Nicole, who'd talked her into this vacation in the first place.

"This place was your idea. I'm down here out of the fire, but you want me to jump back into the flames." She shook her head. "I'll think about it and let you know before you leave."

Nicole stood up. "Okay, do that. I need to run and get with the family. You know how it is. I'll holler back at y'all."

Tayler walked over and gave her friend a hug. "Nicole, don't get me wrong. It does sound like an exciting opportunity."

"Think about the publicity after you're promoted. It's a win-win situation."

Nicole gave Rollin a hug as she stepped off the porch. "Later, peoples. Y'all have a blessed day, and don't do anything I wouldn't do."

Rollin's arms hung at his sides as he continued down the stairs with a slack expression on his face. He headed around the side of the house. After Nicole pulled off, Tayler called out to him.

"Where are you going?"

"I've got work to do," he muttered.

The next morning after breakfast, Rollin and his crew went to the farmer's market, but they didn't ask Tayler if she wanted to go. She'd enjoyed her last trip and had wanted to see what the Saturday morning crowd was like. However, ever since Nicole's visit, something in the air had changed.

Later in the evening, Tayler brought her laptop into the library to look up the Ladies of Distinction organization.

A few minutes later, Rollin walked in.

"Are you ready to eat?"

She looked up. "Are you cooking tonight?"

"No, Rita is, but if you're ready she can prepare everything and go home early. I don't want her to overdo it."

"Sure, I'm ready."

He stared at her for a few seconds before saying, "Nicole shows up and you start working again."

"I'm not really working. Just doing a little research."

He walked over to her and looked down at the computer screen. "You're ready to get out of here, huh?"

"No, that's not it. But I'm leaving in a few weeks, anyway."

He reached out and stroked her cheek with the back of his hand. "Don't remind me."

"But if I decide to help her, I should leave on Monday."

He dropped his hand and looked away. "You're going, aren't you?"

She shrugged. "I don't know. Do you want me to stay?"

He crossed his arms and cocked his head. "What do you think?"

"I think if you want me to stay, you need to say so."

He shook his head and backed away. "It's not my place to tell you to stay or go. You're a grown woman."

"I know I'm grown. I didn't need you to tell me that."

He held up his hands. "Do whatever you want. Like you said, you're leaving in a few weeks anyway, right?"

She watched him back out of the room, shrugging as if he didn't care what she did. She'd wanted him to ask her to stay. No, she wanted him to *beg* her to stay. She needed to know that the love they'd made meant something to him. As it had to her.

Rollin walked back into the kitchen and grabbed a bottle of water from the refrigerator. He closed the door harder than he'd intended.

Rita turned from the sink, where she stood washing dishes. "Don't take it out on the refrigerator."

He swallowed a gulp of water. "Don't take what out on the refrigerator?"

"You know what I'm talking about."

He backed against the counter and crossed his ankles.

"She's a guest, Rollin."

"I know that."

"Then why are you trying to beat up the refrigerator?"

He laughed. "I'll never understand women."

"And I'll never understand why you moved her into a room next to yours when you knew you were attracted to her."

He snorted. "It wasn't my idea."

"Then you let her set you up."

"Yeah, like a fool." He took another swig of water.

"No, baby. Fools don't get their hearts broken."

He almost spit up. "It was not that serious."

Rita stopped, grabbed a towel and turned to Rollin. "Did you forget who you're talking to? I know you, baby. I know you don't open up to people the way you've opened up to Tayler. If she was just another guest, she wouldn't have been sharing your bed every night."

He lowered his water and stared off at the floor.

"It's a dangerous game you started playing. You're gambling with your heart, and from the looks of things, not winning."

He took a deep breath. "So what do I do?"

"Let her know how you feel."

He laughed and shook his head.

"Suit yourself, but you'll never know how she feels until you share your feelings."

He finished off his water and pitched the bottle into the recycling bin next to the back door. If Tayler had any real feelings for him, she would have told him by now. They'd spent every night lying in each other's arms and not once had she expressed any sort of love for him.

"She's ready for dinner, so you can cook and leave early tonight."

Rita gave him a sad smile. "Yes, sir."

He walked out of the kitchen and out the back door. He'd have to chalk Tayler up to a lovely diversion. She'd kept him from focusing on his Whole Foods deal, and he didn't have any more time to waste on her. He didn't care if she left tomorrow or Monday. The sooner she got out of his life, the better. He didn't know if his heart could take her staying much longer.

"Girl, we work good together," Corra said, as she and Tayler put the finishing touches on the fund-raiser. "I can't wait for the night of the ceremony. The school board is so excited about the money we've collected so far."

"So am I," Tayler admitted. "If we'd had more time I think we could have equipped every classroom."

"This is so freaking exciting. Even Rollin gave us a donation."

"That's great."

"Thank you for working with him on this. You guys are going to look great up there together as MCs."

"Is that what we're doing?" Tayler was discovering that Corra was a pro at leaving out details, just like Nicole.

"Yes, I didn't tell you?"

Tayler laughed. "No, you didn't."

"Well, I need you guys to introduce me and read off all the sponsors. You know how they like to be recognized in front of everyone. Plus, if I put Rollin's name on the flyer as MC, I'm guaranteed a big crowd of females."

Tayler laughed. "So why don't you MC with Rollin—a brother-and-sister team?"

"No, I need to be announced. And Rollin and I would probably get into an argument up there. People don't need to see that. Besides, you two look good together. You're two very attractive people who obviously have the hots for each other."

Shocked that Corra had detected anything between them, Tayler played dumb.

"Corra, there's nothing between me and Rollin." Tayler hated to lie to Corra, but she had to.

"I hear you, but I know what I see. Rollin hasn't had that goofy grin plastered on his face for weeks for nothing. If there's nothing between you two, there should be. He's a good man, and I know he cares about you."

Tayler thought about what Corra said all the way back to the B and B. From Nicole this morning to Corra this afternoon, everyone was seeing what she hadn't wanted them to see. How come she couldn't have sex with that man without getting all emotionally involved? How come she couldn't just go back to Chicago with beautiful memories of a wonderful man? Instead of falling in love with him.

* * *

She walked into the B and B brain tired and ready to take a nap before dinner. The house was quiet. She proceeded down the hall and opened the door to her room. Something didn't feel right. She didn't see her suitcase against the wall where she'd left it. She walked over and opened the closet door. It was empty.

"What the hell is going on?" Could someone have come in and stolen her clothes? She stormed out of the room in search of Rollin or Rita. In the kitchen, she noticed Rita had prepared dinner and left everything on the stove. That meant Rollin wasn't too far away, since he would be serving dinner.

When she walked back out into the hallway, Rollin was coming down the stairs.

"Rollin, what happened to my things?"

"They're upstairs in your room."

She looked at him surprised. "Oh, you moved me back upstairs?"

"Yeah, hope you don't mind. You weren't using the room downstairs, anyway. I don't think I forgot anything, but you can double-check."

"You could have waited until I got back, you know."

He continued down the stairs and past her. "I needed to get it over with. I've got a busy evening."

First her eyes followed him as he walked into the kitchen. What the hell had gotten into him? Then she followed him. The minute she reached out for the kitchen door, it opened and she fell forward into Rollin's chest.

"I'm sorry," she said as she caught herself. His body remained stiff and he didn't touch her.

"Dinner's ready. I've set the table. You can have a seat."

He looked at her with a blank expression on his face. She turned around and saw one place setting. He wouldn't be joining her.

"What happened to the music this evening?" There was always music playing from the library. Lately, it had been their favorite R&B choices.

"I didn't put any on."

"Mind if I do?" she asked.

He shrugged and turned to walk out. "Help yourself."

She went into the library and fished around until she found the Maxwell CD.

When she returned he'd placed the food on the table, but Rollin was nowhere around. She sat down and fixed her plate. He walked in.

"Got everything you need?" he asked sternly.

She looked around the table. "How about sweetener for my tea?"

He went into the kitchen and returned with a container of sweeteners.

"And how about some lemon for my tea?"

He frowned, but turned around and went back into the kitchen. Tayler knew she was messing with him, but couldn't help herself. He needed to lighten up.

He returned with a saucer of sliced lemons and set them in front of her. "Is that enough?"

She snapped her fingers. "Damn, Rollin, I forgot to ask you for some—"

He leaned over, placing both hands on the table, and stared at her. "Tayler, let's not play this game."

"Then tell me what's wrong with you."

He straightened up. "There's nothing wrong with me. Do you need anything else for dinner?"

She looked up at him with a wicked grin on her face. "Can I have anything I want?"

He chuckled and rubbed the back of his neck. "Look I don't have time for you to play with me tonight. I've got work to do. Just leave your dishes on the table when you finish." Then he turned to walk out.

"Rollin, I haven't been playing with you. We're grown and knew what we were getting into, right?"

He stopped and looked back at her. "Yeah, we just had a little fun, right?" he asked, his words dripping with sarcasm.

Chapter 17

Tayler woke up Sunday morning with a decision to make. Was she leaving Monday or not? After breakfast she rode out with Kevin, thinking about how much she would miss these morning rides. They were a part of her routine now.

Rita had invited her to church, and she took her up on the invitation. In church she ran into so many people she'd met over the last couple of weeks. Corra and Rollin were there, but Rollin managed to keep his distance. Still upset, she assumed.

After church, she helped Rita out in the gardens, the whole time contemplating whether or not she should stay. She mentally weighed the pros and cons of her departure. Participation would mean a lot to the Color of Success, but leaving so soon would hurt any chance of building upon what she'd started with Rollin.

She felt all alone in her decision process.

"You're awful quiet this afternoon," Rita said as Tayler placed another long-stem rose in the basket she held.

"I'm sorry. I have a lot on my mind today," Tayler said.

"Did you enjoy the service this morning? I thought the reverend did an exceptional job today."

Tayler slipped her hands into her back pockets. "I really enjoyed it. The service reminded me of going to church with my grandmother in Rockford, Illinois, when I was a little girl. And I hadn't thought about that in years."

"Is that where your family's from?"

"Some of them. We're pretty much scattered all over the globe, though."

Rita smiled and took the shears from Tayler. "That's enough flowers. I'm getting ready for a couple of guests tomorrow."

"That's great," Tayler said in reply.

"Wallace will be back to pick me up in a minute for afternoon service. Are you going to be okay here alone?" Rita asked.

"I'll be fine. I'm sure Rollin will be around somewhere."

"You know, Tayler, Rollin's not a perfect man. And one of his major flaws is his inability to deal with his feelings. Right now, he's hurt pretty bad and he doesn't know how to express it."

"How did I hurt him?"

"He gave you his heart, and he doesn't do that often."

"What do you mean?"

Rita smiled. "I've said too much already. Why don't you talk to Rollin?"

"I would, but he won't talk to me. I'd hate to leave with us not speaking."

"So, you're going back tomorrow with Nicole?"

"I haven't made up my mind yet. But I won't leave without letting you know."

"Well, I hope you decide to stay, but if you don't, please talk to Rollin before you go."

"I'll try to."

When Rita left, Tayler was in the library balled up on the couch listening to love music and wishing Rollin was there with her. She must have dozed off, because she woke to the sound of someone in the kitchen. She got up and stretched. The music had stopped and it was dark outside.

She found Rollin in the kitchen fixing himself something to eat. She stood in the doorway for a few minutes without saying a word. He looked up and noticed her.

"Can I get you something?" he asked in a businesslike tone.

"Yeah," she said and walked on in. "An explanation."

He turned away from her and poured his drink down the sink. "For what?"

"For starters, your funky attitude. Ever since Nicole's visit, you've treated me horribly. What did I do to you?"

"If my attitude has been less than hospitable, I apologize."

"Don't give me that bull. After spending nights in

your bed, I think I deserve to be treated better than a guest, don't you?"

"After spending nights in my bed, I wouldn't expect you to be eager to leave, either."

"Rollin, you knew there was a possibility I'd leave after a month. I've been here three weeks. Regardless, I wasn't staying longer than two months anyway. As much as I like it here, I do have a job to go back to."

"So why wait? Leave tomorrow with Nicole. I'll be glad to refund you for the nights you don't stay."

"I don't need a freakin' refund—you can keep the money. What pisses me off is how you act like what we shared meant nothing to you. Maybe that was your plan all along. Huh? Is that what you do, romance the guest and have them spend time in the proprietor's bed? Then you get Rita on your side to make you appear to be such a good guy."

Rollin paced the kitchen floor, rubbing his hand across his close-cut hair.

Tayler didn't care if what she said hurt him or not now, she was pissed beyond belief. "Or maybe you and Corra set this whole thing up. Is that why she never comes over? You probably asked her not to, planning to seduce me the whole time."

He stopped and snapped on her. "Seduce you! What the hell are you talking about? All I had to do was touch you, and you gushed like a river. I wouldn't be surprised if you hadn't planned to seduce me. Maybe you and Nicole set this whole thing up."

"Don't be ridiculous."

He frowned. "Don't you be ridiculous. I'm running a business here. I don't go around sleeping with my guests. If I did, do you think I'd still be in business?"

She threw her hand up in the air. "Oh, so how did I get so lucky?"

He pounded his fist against the countertop.

She jumped.

"From the minute you stepped out of the car that first day, I knew I was in trouble. Now I'm tripping because I'm too emotionally involved to pretend you don't mean anything to me. But all I can do is stand back and let you leave. That pisses me off," he yelled.

"And you think it doesn't bother me?" she shouted back.

"It must not. You just roll in here, break a brother's heart and go on your merry way."

"Rollin, what was I supposed to do? I tried avoiding you, but that didn't work." Couldn't he see the situation she was in?

"Just what you did—nothing. Go back to Chicago. Nicole needs you." He turned around and stormed out the back door.

Tayler stood there staring at the door. Then what he'd just said hit her like a ton of bricks and she ran to the back door. He was gone.

He'd fallen in love with her, and she'd broken his heart.

"Honey, I wish you'd wait for Rollin to get back before you leave." Rita wrung her hands over and over as she tried to get Tayler to stick around until Rollin and Kevin returned from the fields that morning.

"I can't, Rita. He made it pretty clear last night that he wanted me to leave."

Tayler had packed and called Nicole, and she was

ready to hit the road. She only hated that she wouldn't get to see Corra one last time before she left.

"Well, you be careful. That's a long drive."

"I will," Tayler said.

Rita pulled her into an embrace and Tayler felt as if her heart was shrinking. Through watery eyes she watched Wallace walk out onto the porch with his head down.

"We're sure going to miss you," Rita said after letting her go. "Your stay was the longest we've ever had. I feel like you're a part of the family now."

Tayler's heart broke a little more. Wallace walked over to give her a bear hug. "Let me grab that for you," he said and took her suitcase out to the car.

"Tell Rollin I'll call him."

Rita nodded. "Give him a little time—he'll come around."

Minutes later, Tayler was riding out of Danville with tears in her eyes when she passed a black monster truck that resembled Rollin's going in the opposite direction. She looked in her rearview mirror, but the truck kept going.

Rollin stood outside Corra's door and knocked for the third time. He could have rung the doorbell or used his key, but he didn't want to wake or startle the kids, so he kept knocking. The porch lights finally came on. It was late. Too late to be here, he now realized.

The door swung open and Corra peeked out in her robe with a purple bonnet on her head. "Rollin, what's wrong?"

"I need to talk to you," he said and walked in past her.

"Don't you know what time it is? It's after ten and

you'll wake the kids." She closed the front door and followed him into the den.

"I'm sorry, but you'll have to find someone else to MC the fund-raiser." He sat down and raked his hand down his face, tired from the couple of beers he'd had since he found out Tayler left.

"What do you mean, I need to find someone else?" she asked, flopping down across the couch from him.

"Tayler's gone."

"Gone where? Rollin, what are you talking about? I've told everybody you're going to be the MC. You and Tayler are a team. I need you guys."

Rollin stood up and scanned the semidark den. "Didn't you hear me? She's gone back to Chicago. She left this morning."

Corra stood up. "What! Why? What did you say to her, Rollin?"

Rollin dropped his head and grabbed his temples to stop the pounding in his head. "I don't know why I came all the way over here. I could have just called you."

"So there was something going on between you and Tayler?" she asked with such enthusiasm he was certain now that he'd made a mistake.

"Yes, and no." He walked over to pick up the TV remote.

"Then give me a good reason why she left before the fund-raiser ceremony, and without calling me."

"She went back to work on some conference with Nicole. Her vacation's over."

"But I thought she was staying two months? We already mapped the whole program out with you and her as MCs."

"Well, she won't be here." He turned on the TV.

"I knew there was something going on between you two. Rollin, what did you do or say to her?"

"I didn't do anything." *That's the problem. I didn't stop her from leaving. I encouraged it.*

"You have real feelings for Tayler, I know, and she has feelings for you. It could have been the start of something beautiful."

He laughed and headed for the door. "That's what I thought, too, but instead of it being the start of something, it was just a summer fling."

"You don't know that. Is that what she said?"

"She didn't have to. She left." He opened the door and stepped outside.

"Rollin, you're my brother and I love you, but you are the most stubborn man there is. If you don't show up for the fund-raiser, look for yourself another family. The kids and I will disown you, and that's all there is to it." She slammed the door behind him.

Chapter 18

A few days in Chicago and Tayler was back in the rat race. Although she'd resisted the temptation to open her email and check on work, she'd been running all over town with Nicole working on the conference. After a meeting with the Ladies of Distinction to discuss conference logistics turned into an episode of *The Real Housewives of Anywhere*, Tayler had to ask herself why she was doing this.

At night she lay in bed unable to sleep or get Rollin off her mind. She wanted to call him, or hoped that he'd break down and call her. But she knew he wouldn't. He was in love with her! She said it over and over again. He was in love with her, and she was in love with him. So why were they so many miles apart?

She needed to talk to somebody, and finally decided it was time to share her feelings with Nicole. Even if it were eleven o'clock at night. She dialed her best friend.

"Tayler, it's so funny you should call me, because I was thinking about calling you. But I thought you might be asleep, so I said, 'I'll call her in the morning.'"

"I can't sleep," Tayler admitted.

"Why, what's wrong? Hey, if it's about the meeting, don't worry, they don't always act like that. You'd think educated women with money would have more class."

"Nicole, it's not that."

"What is it then?"

"I don't want back into the rat race."

"What rat race? You won't be working the conference alone. We'll have a whole slew of women helping out. I've got volunteers from Columbia, too. It won't be as hard as—"

"Wait a minute…you aren't hearing me. I don't just mean the conference. I mean everything."

"Hold on, let me turn this damned television down. I didn't understand that." She briefly put down the phone.

Tayler leaned back against the headboard and took a deep breath. If anyone would understand what she was about to say, it was Nicole.

"Okay, let's have that again."

"I've given it a lot of thought and I don't know if I want the director position after all."

"Tayler, did you fall off a tractor or something and bump your head? What the hell are you talking about, you don't want that position? You've been working toward it since you joined MesaCom."

"I know, but suddenly it just doesn't seem that important anymore."

"Tayler…no, that can't be."

Tayler didn't say anything.

"Girl, you didn't go down there and fall in love with my cousin, did you?"

A tear rolled down Tayler's cheek. "Nicole, I don't know how it happened. One night I was complaining about him being so rude and obnoxious, then the next I was in his bed and didn't want to leave his arms."

A loud scream came from the other end of the phone. Tayler yanked the receiver back. She hadn't expected that type of reaction.

"I knew it. That's all I'm saying, I knew it. You know you can't keep anything from me. I could see it all over your face when I was over there. And the look on Rollin's face when I mentioned you returning to Chicago was priceless."

The tears flowed down Tayler's cheeks. "Nicole, what am I going to do? You got me into this mess."

"Me? I sent you there to get some rest, not to jump in bed with the man. What was it like?"

"Nicole!"

"Oh, never mind, he's my cousin. I don't want to know."

"That's nasty, girl."

"Hell, I didn't need to ask anyway—you're talking about passing up a plum promotion. He must be working with a magic stick or something."

"It's not just him. It's the B and B, the town, Corra, Rita, all of the above. I fell in love with your family."

"Are you telling me three weeks in the country changed your perspective on life?"

"Yes, I think so. Now tell me what to do."

"Damn, Tayler. Well, you know I'm here for you. What do you want to do?"

"I don't know. I can't concentrate on anything. Not even the conference. I want to be with Rollin."

"Then pack your shit up and head back to Kentucky. That's all I know to tell you."

Tayler woke bright and early Thursday morning to visit her favorite boutique on Michigan Avenue. She needed two jaw-dropping gowns for the fund-raiser ceremony. She didn't like the way she'd left Corra hanging, but this should make it up to her. After she picked up the gowns she met Nicole at Water Tower Place for lunch.

"Are you sure about this?" Nicole asked.

Tayler shook her head. "No, I'm not sure about anything. I have no idea how Rollin's going to respond when he sees me. But I have to go back and find out. If it's not meant to be, I can always come home and go back to work."

"And if it does work out?"

Tayler smiled. "Then I'll be home."

Nicole reached across the table for Tayler's hand. "What can I do to help you?"

"The *Housewives* are going to need a new speaker for their conference." Both Tayler and Nicole laughed. "I was thinking about the president of the Color of Success," Tayler said.

Nicole's eyes widened and she let go of Tayler's hand. "You're the motivational speaker, not me."

"Don't you think it's about time the president of the Color of Success started representing the organization? You've led just as many workshops as I have, and you're passionate about the work. You'd make a great motivational speaker."

Nicole kept shaking her head while rolling her eyes. "No, no. I don't have the same stage presence or timing or anything that you have."

"Nicole, give in now, because I'm going to talk you into it the same way you talked me into vacationing at Coleman House."

Nicole took a deep breath. "I guess it's time for me to put my big-girl britches on, huh?"

Tayler smiled at her friend, who had more potential than she knew.

Tayler rolled into Danville Saturday afternoon and drove straight to Corra's house. Several cars were parked outside, but thankfully she didn't see Rollin's truck. She parked and walked to the front door, not knowing what type of reception she would get. Would Corra be mad at her? Or would she welcome her back? There was only one way to find out. She rang the bell and stood back.

Corra opened the door with her head turned, yelling at the kids. When she turned around and saw Tayler, a big smile broke out on her face and she threw the screen door open.

"Tayler, girl, I'm so happy to see you. Get in here."

Tayler walked in and greeted her friend with a big hug.

"What happened? Why did you leave? Why did you come back? Oh, my God, I'm so glad you're here." Corra stopped yapping and hugged Tayler again.

Tayler couldn't get a word in.

Corra closed the door. "Sharon, look who's here."

A woman walked out of the kitchen and looked down the split-level entrance at Tayler and Corra standing just inside the door.

"It's Tayler. Our MC. She's back," Corra said, beaming.

Sharon threw the index cards she had in her hand up in the air. "Thank God. I couldn't remember all that stuff."

Tayler turned to Corra. "She was going to replace you. Come on in and tell me everything. What happened?"

"First, I've got something for you. It's in the car—I'll be right back." Tayler ran out to the car and brought in the gowns and her overnight bag.

All the fund-raiser committee members in the house gathered around the living room sofa as Tayler unzipped the garment bag and pulled out the gown. She had picked out a strapless white-and-gold gown with a corseted bodice, which should fit even if the size was off a bit. It was adorned with gorgeous jeweled lace appliqué and a flowing skirt that was sheer past midthigh.

"I'm so sorry I left the way I did, but I hope this more than makes up for it." She handed Corra the dress.

Corra's jaw dropped.

After all the crying and screaming they sat down and went over last-minute changes to the program.

Before they left for the venue, Corra pulled Tayler aside. "I'm so happy to see you, but Rollin will be happier than I am. He might not show it right away. He's stubborn like that."

"Don't I know," Tayler said.

"I don't know what happened between you two, but I know he loves you. Have you spoken to him?"

Tayler shook her head. "No. I wanted my return to be a surprise."

Corra tilted her head and gave Tayler a thumbs-up. "Good move."

Tayler entered the auditorium more nervous than she had ever been when preparing to stand before a crowd. She'd helped Corra create a script for her and Rollin, but she wasn't sure he'd even read it.

"Tayler! Honey, I'm so glad to see you. You look absolutely gorgeous." Rita and Wallace approached Tayler with smiles and hugs.

"I'm glad to see you, too." Tayler had chosen a one-shoulder mermaid-style red satin gown and a pair of black stilettos that she hoped would knock Rollin off his feet.

"Thank you so much for coming back to help Corra out. You ladies gave this fund-raiser the boost it needed to get computers into almost every classroom."

"I hope so," Tayler said, really wanting that statement to be true.

Rita looked around. "Have you seen Rollin?"

"No, I haven't. He is coming, isn't he?" Tayler asked.

"He'd better show up. He promised Corra," Rita said.

"Yeah, well, we all know how hardheaded Rollin can be," Wallace added.

The door to the auditorium opened with a loud squeak and everyone turned around as Rollin walked in. When she saw him, dressed in a perfectly tailored slate-gray suit and dark shades, Tayler's heart stopped. He held the door for an attractive woman Tayler was sure she'd seen around town before. Had he shown up to the ceremony with a date?

Rita crossed her arms, and Wallace cleared his throat. Tayler didn't wait for Rollin to flaunt his date in her face.

"Excuse me. I think I'll see if Corra needs my help." Before she walked off backstage, Rollin removed his shades and made eye contact with her. His eyes traveled down her body before she turned her head and swished across the room. She wanted him to see what he was missing.

Five minutes before the curtains opened, Rollin made his way backstage.

"It's about time," Corra said with a disgusted tone to her voice. "Tell me you read your script and know what to do?"

"Yeah, I read it."

"Good, then let's get this show on the road. Look who's back." Corra pointed to Tayler before going off to check on the entertainment.

Rollin walked over to Tayler as she pretended to refresh her memory by reading the index cards. Since she'd written the script, she knew everything by heart, but he didn't know that.

"I didn't think I'd ever see you again," he said.

She nodded. "You did tell me to go back to Chicago, remember?"

"You were ready to go. I didn't see any reason to prolong the agony."

"Whose, yours or mine?" she asked.

His chin dropped to his chest. She wanted to talk to

him, but this was neither the place nor the time. Why were men so stubborn?

"Who's your date?" she asked.

He glanced behind him. "My what?"

"Okay, you guys, it's showtime." Corra ran up, clapping her hands. "Come on, let's get this show on the road."

She pushed Rollin and Tayler toward the stage. The job of MC wasn't hard for Tayler. However, the spotlight was new to Rollin and he didn't seem as comfortable onstage as she did. He did however, stick to the script for the most part, and she was glad about that.

After a young girl's musical performance, Rollin took to the stage to welcome everyone and remind them of the silent auction going on in the next room. "Be sure to place your bids—the auction will be concluding in about an hour from now."

The woman he'd walked in with shouted out, "Can I bid on you?"

The audience laughed and applauded as a few other women shouted out that they wanted in on that bidding.

"That's not the type of auction we're having this afternoon. Today's all about— "

"Oh, we know what it's about. But if y'all really want to raise some money, let me bid on a night out with you."

Tayler lowered her head and laughed while the audience seemed to get a kick out of Rollin's discomfort. When she glanced over at him he tilted his head toward her and pleaded silently for help. Help that she wasn't about to give him. She shook her head.

"Come on, Rollin. I've got fifty dollars for a date."

"I've got one hundred," another woman shouted out.

"Ladies, ladies, come on, that's funny, but let's get back to the program." He tried, but he'd lost complete control of the situation. Most of the crowd laughed and applauded while others shook their heads.

Finally Tayler decided to step in and help him out. She took the microphone. "Ladies, you know we are still short of our goal and I think that's an excellent idea. So how about we add a date with Danville's most eligible bachelor to the program?" She pointed to Rollin, who looked as if someone had just sucker punched him right in the gut.

Corra stood up and led the audience in a round of applause and laughter.

Rollin shook his head and held a hand up as he backed up.

"Come on, ladies, what do you say, can we talk him into it?" Tayler encouraged the audience. She joined them in a round of applause and motioned for Rollin to step up to the mic.

He glared at her as if he wanted to kill her, but then gave in with a quick smile. Tayler stepped back. Everything was in control again, or so she thought.

"I'll tell you what," he said, leaning into the microphone. "I'll auction myself off if you do the same?" he asked, looking back at Tayler.

She was mortified.

Chapter 19

Several men in the audience took to their feet, clapping and whistling. What was Rollin doing? To auction him off was another way to make a couple hundred dollars. They didn't need to turn this into a sideshow.

"Come on, let's hear it. Who wants a date with the lovely Ms. Tayler Carter from big-city Chicago?" Rollin led a round of applause and motioned for Tayler to take the microphone.

She didn't move. How could he do this to her? She must have looked like a deer caught in the headlights, because Rollin was thoroughly amused.

Corra sat in the front row clapping the loudest.

Tayler regained her composure. She admired Rollin's ability to regain control over the audience so fast. She stepped back up to the microphone.

"If there's one thing I love, it's a good challenge."

The audience went wild with applause and whistles. More people entered the room and the crowd grew.

"So, how shall we do this?" Tayler asked, looking at Corra.

Corra stood up and hurried to the stage. She happily took the microphone. "I'll take it from here."

Tayler and Rollin stepped aside while Corra did her thing. This was her crowd and she knew how to work them up before opening the bidding.

"That was cute," Rollin mumbled and glared at Tayler.

"Yes, a nice comeback on your part as well," she hissed back at him.

"You liked that, huh?" he asked in a whisper.

"Not actually, but what choice did I have?" She smiled and kept her eyes on the audience.

"Now you know how I felt."

Corra started the bidding with Rollin. "Let's start the bid at fifty dollars for dinner with Rollin Coleman, owner and operator of Coleman House B and B and Coleman Organic Farm. Ladies, you know some of y'all been chasing him all over town—this is your opportunity to have him all to yourself for one precious evening."

Tayler grinned. This makeshift auction really was Corra's thing. She knew how to hype the women up into a frenzy.

"I'm glad you think this is so funny," Rollin whispered.

"It's hilarious," Tayler said between clenched teeth.

Rollin stood with his hands behind his back while Corra walked over and tried to get him to flex his muscles. He laughed but refused. The woman who'd arrived at the same time as Rollin placed a one-hundred-dollar bid.

"Wow, looks like she really wants you. I guess one night wasn't enough," Tayler whispered out of the side of her mouth.

"What are you talking about?" Rollin whispered.

"Your date," Tayler responded with a smile.

"Can I get one twenty-five?" Corra called out.

Rollin turned to Tayler and crossed his arms. "I didn't bring a date."

"Oh, so what did you guys do? Conveniently bump into each other outside?" She crossed her arms and looked everywhere but at him.

"Who? What are you talking about? I came here by myself." He had stopped whispering.

Tayler cut her eyes at him. "You didn't walk in by yourself."

Corra turned around and gave them a stern look. "Are you guys okay?" she asked.

Rollin nodded. "Yeah, we're cool."

Corra turned back to the auction. "I'm looking for one twenty-five, ladies."

Rollin dropped his arms and shoved his hands into his pants pockets. "What do you care if I brought someone or not? Your vacation's over and you had your fun." He lowered his voice but still wasn't whispering.

The bidding reached $150, and Rollin turned to smile at the audience, displaying those big dimples.

"That wasn't fair," Tayler said.

Excited now, Corra was all over the stage. "Can

I get two hundred? Come on, ladies, we need computers."

"Life isn't fair," Rollin continued. "If it was, you wouldn't have done what you did."

Tayler crossed her arms again and took a step toward Rollin. "What did I do?"

"Shh—what is wrong with you guys?" Corra snapped at them.

"I'm sorry." Tayler turned around and tried to smile.

"You know what you did," he replied.

"Sold, to Tina Smith in the striking purple dress for one hundred seventy-five dollars. You go, girl."

"If anything, you did something to me," Tayler retorted.

"Okay, fellas, your turn. How about a date with the beautiful Tayler Carter?"

Rollin chuckled out loud. "Naw, baby, don't try to turn this around. You walked into my life and flipped the switch."

"Tayler is vice president at MesaCom Telecommunications in Chicago. She's also an internationally known motivational speaker. Let's start the bid at one hundred dollars."

Tayler couldn't believe Rollin had the audacity to say what he had. "Huh—you couldn't keep your hands off me. How dare you play the victim? I'm not some heartless bitch."

"Tayler!" Corra shouted in a deep voice.

Tayler snapped her head around to see Corra and half the audience staring at her. She'd stopped whispering.

"Maybe they should bid on each other," a man on the front row shouted out, and everyone laughed.

* * *

Tayler sat backstage after the ceremony wishing the ground would open and swallow her whole.

"Don't worry about it, baby. Half the audience didn't hear you, anyway," Rita assured her.

"But half of them did, and they were children." She buried her face in the palm of her hands. She couldn't shake the horrified looks on the parents' faces.

"What were you two arguing about, anyway?" Rita asked.

Tayler shook her head. Seeing Rollin walk in with another woman had started it all. "He denied he'd come with a date."

"A date? Who did he bring with him?" Rita asked.

"I don't know, whoever that woman was that he walked in with. I'm gone one week and he starts dating somebody."

Rita held a hand to her chest laughing. "Bernice? Oh, my goodness, you thought he was with Bernice."

"That's her name. I remember her from the farmer's market. She was flirting with Rollin."

"Honey, Bernice flirts with every single man in town. He wasn't with her. They just arrived at the same time."

A jealous lover was not the role Tayler wanted to play. Her chest caved as she covered her face with her hands.

"You okay?" Corra asked and sat down beside Tayler.

"Corra I am so sorry. I don't know what got into me. I ruined the fund-raiser."

"What? No, you didn't. Greg paid two hundred dollars for a date with you. Counting the one seventy-five we got for Rollin, we made another three hundred seventy-five dollars. Then Pastor Richardson offered to match that. Girl, this auction idea was ingenious. We raised enough to purchase another computer."

Tayler reached out and grabbed Corra by the shoulders. "Say that again."

Corra laughed. "Yes, another computer. It was a success."

Tayler let out a heavy sigh. "Thank God." The only problem was, now she had to go on a date with Greg.

As the evening wound down, more parents thanked Tayler than turned away from her. Tonight, she felt like a part of the community. Rita and Wallace decided to call it a night and head back to Garrard County.

Tayler and Corra stood around talking when a tall handsome man with that boy-next-door look walked up behind Corra and cleared his throat.

Corra turned around. "Chris! I'm so glad you made it."

His eyes sparkled as he looked at Corra as if he were seeing her for the first time.

"I wouldn't have missed it. And you look great, by the way."

"Thank you."

Tayler smiled as they stood there admiring one another and ignoring her.

"Hi, I'm Tayler." She stuck her hand out and introduced herself when their conversation subsided.

"Oh, God, I'm so sorry." Corra pressed her hands to her cheeks before introducing Tayler and Chris. Tayler was so happy she'd purchased that gown for Corra—she looked like a million bucks. Minutes later, Tayler excused herself and left them smiling at one another.

"Well, that didn't turn out too bad," Rollin said as he came up behind her.

Tayler was still embarrassed and didn't know what to say to him. She'd made a fool of herself onstage before the entire community. "No, I guess not."

"Don't look so sad. Most of the crowd thought we were acting to drum up the bids."

"But we know better."

Two young women passing by smiled and waved. "That was a great program, guys."

Rollin gave them a slight nod of the head. "Thank you." Then he turned back to Tayler. "I don't know who you thought I brought with me, but I came alone."

"I know better now. I'm sorry. I stood up there and made a complete fool of myself."

"No, you didn't. You just looked like a jealous girlfriend."

He stared down at her and bit his bottom lip. He looked so sexy she wanted to reach up and wrap her arms around his neck and kiss him right now.

"I wasn't trying to break your heart."

"I know you weren't. I've had to come to grips with my own feelings and not be mad at myself for falling in love with you so fast." He let out a heavy sigh. "So did you just come back for the ceremony, or do you plan to stay a little while?"

She shrugged. "That all depends."

"On what?" he asked.

"Here you are." Corra, Chris and a few committee members walked up. "I told you guys I had the right MCs, didn't I?" she asked, looking from Tayler to Rollin as they stood up.

"Come on, give me some credit here. The way you

turned the second half of the program into a money-maker—I never would have thought of that."

Tayler looked at Rollin and shrugged. "It wasn't really our idea. Somebody in the audience started it."

"Yeah, girl, but you took it and ran with it. That's the type of energy and creativity we need around here. And now it's time to celebrate." Corra threw her hands up in the air and sashayed around in her new gown. "The party's at my house and everybody's welcome. I've got plenty of food, and drinks. Jamie and Katie are staying with their babysitter, Mrs. Baker, tonight. So we can party the night away.

Corra was excited, and Rollin was excited for her. She and her small committee had done a lot of work to get computers into more than half of the classrooms at Roosevelt Elementary. She deserved to party a little bit.

Rollin caught Kevin walking around and gave him his keys, trusting him to get his truck home.

He took Tayler's keys and helped her into the passenger's side of her BMW. For the first time he realized there was a lot he still didn't know about her. He climbed in behind the wheel and started the car.

"In case I didn't tell you, you look stunning." Red was her color, he concluded.

"Thank you."

"So, what happened with the work on the conference?"

"I decided something else was more important. The past few weeks have meant a lot to me. I'd never wanted to be with any man more than I wanted to be with you that first night. What we had was more than a vacation fling for me, but I didn't know how to deal with it, either. It happened so fast that it caught me off guard. Then, before I knew it, you turned on me."

"I was hurt. It was stupid, I know, but when you didn't say anything to Nicole about us, that hurt."

"At the time I didn't know how or what to tell her."

"You could have told her the truth."

"What, that I'd fallen in love with her cousin in three weeks?"

Rollin pulled to a stop at a stop sign and turned to Tayler and smiled. "You what?"

Tayler bit her lip and shrugged. "I tried not to, but you made it nearly impossible with those big dimples."

He laughed. "Is that all it was? My dimples?"

She shrugged. "Maybe a little more than that."

As soon as he pulled out and rounded the bend headed toward town, his cell phone rang.

"Hello."

"Rollin, it's Greg."

Rollin's supposed buddy who'd paid two hundred dollars for a date with Tayler was calling him. Rollin's first inclination was to hang up, but there was a catch in Greg's voice that didn't sound right.

"What's up?"

"Man, you need to get over to the Danville county hospital. Corra was in an accident."

Rollin almost slammed on the brakes. "She what?"

"Yeah, man, they got hit by some kid driving drunk."

"Is she going to be okay?"

"I think so."

"Thanks, Greg."

Rollin hung up, threw his phone into the middle

console and turned the BMW around in the middle of the road.

"What's wrong?" she asked, holding on.

"Corra's in the hospital. They were hit by a drunk driver."

"Oh, no!" Tayler braced her hand against the dashboard.

Rollin gunned the sporty car down a shortcut and said a silent prayer that both Corra and Chris were okay. The mere mention of the words—*car accident* and *hospital*—reminded him of when his parents died. He had to get to Corra, because he knew she was probably freaking out. Dying in a car accident was the one thing that scared her.

They reached the hospital and Rollin pulled into the emergency area and jumped out of the car. He helped Tayler out and they ran inside. They approached the nurse behind the emergency room desk and got the details of Corra's surgery. His heart was beating so fast and hard he could hardly hear her. If anything happened to Corra, he didn't know what he'd do. She was all he had left in the world. He squeezed Tayler's hand.

Corra had a bad break to her leg, but she was going to be okay.

The nurse pointed them toward the waiting room. The few people in there looked as if they'd been up all day, while Tayler and Rollin looked as though they were headed to the prom.

He pulled out his cell phone and called Rita and Wallace to tell them about the accident. Then he took off his suit jacket and put it around Tayler shoulders. She shivered as if she was freezing. She leaned her head on his shoulder and he knew instantly that he couldn't let this woman get away. She'd changed his life from the day she walked into it.

Chapter 20

"Rollin, have you called the kids yet?"

"No, not yet. I wanted to make sure Corra's okay first."

"They need to know their mother's all right before they find out she's in the hospital. Don't let them hear it from somebody else."

"I won't."

He wrapped his arm around Tayler's shoulder and kissed the top of her head.

"Let me go check on Corra, and I'll be right back."

After he left, Tayler sat with her arms crossed, holding his jacket around her. She didn't know what to do. She wanted to be with Rollin, but this was crazy—she'd known him less than two months. Yet she was prepared to leave her life in Chicago without the promise of a future with him.

Minutes later, Kevin walked in.

"Rollin called and asked me to come get you and take you over to the B and B. He's gonna stay here until Corra comes out of surgery."

Tayler stood up. "Okay, let's go."

A few hours later, Rollin sat in Corra's semiprivate room. She was a little woozy but she looked good. She tried to sit up in bed but winced from the pain.

"Don't move, girl," Rollin told her. He'd never had a broken leg before, but he knew it had to be painful whether your body was pumped with drugs or not.

"Rollin, how long have I been out?"

"A few hours," he told her.

"Where are Jamie and Katie?"

"I had Kevin pick them up from Mrs. Baker's and carry them over to the house. Tayler's with them."

"How's Chris?"

"He's fine. The doctor said he can see you after I come out. One visitor at a time."

Her head fell back into the pillow. "Oh, man. I feel like I've been run over by a Mack truck."

"Naw, just a drunk teenager in a beat-up Honda."

"Don't make light of my situation."

"I'm not. You're lucky to be alive. I'm glad you're okay."

"So am I. You know, I need to tell you about this dream I had. It was so weird." She reached for the cup of ice on the tray beside her bed.

Rollin grabbed the cup and handed it to her. "When did you have a dream?"

"During surgery, I guess. I don't know, but I was

back at the B and B working along with you and Rita. Mama was there, too."

Rollin sat in the chair next to her bed. "Maybe you bumped your head in the accident, too."

"Maybe so. I don't know, but let me tell you this was more like a vision. Mama was in the kitchen baking cookies. You know, like she used to do whenever we had guests coming. I could smell them—they smelled so good."

Rollin chuckled. "She used to bake the hell out of some cookies, didn't she?"

"Oh, man, I can taste them now. Remember the lemon ones? You used to call them bait cookies because they were so addictive."

He chuckled. "Yeah, I remember."

"Mama was in the kitchen, but Tayler came down the steps from upstairs. She had a bundle of something in her arms. Either she was cleaning one of the rooms, or she had a baby."

He laughed. "Damn, you hit your head really hard, didn't you?"

Corra tried to raise up from her pillow again. "Don't laugh at me. I'm trying to tell you what I saw. Tayler was in the house with us."

"Where was Daddy?"

"I don't know. I didn't see him. But once Tayler entered the kitchen, Mama disappeared." Corra closed her eyes.

"What do you mean, she disappeared?"

"She was no longer there. All I saw was you and Tayler. Then I woke up."

"Okay, you're right. That was a weird dream, probably brought on by the painkillers."

She shook her head. "No, I think it was a vision, like I said. I've never told you this, but I'm so proud of you for keeping the bed-and-breakfast open. I know it's not easy and I haven't been able to help out a lot, but you've kept Mama's dream alive.

"I don't think you should let Tayler go, either. I know you're in love with her, and don't try to deny it. That little spat at the fund-raiser wasn't staged, so don't try to convince me it was."

He couldn't fool Corra and had no intention of trying to. "Okay, so she's grown on me in the last couple of weeks."

Corra laughed and then winced. "Oh, don't make me laugh, it hurts. Vegetables grow on you. Tayler has gotten under your skin and all up in your head. I don't know what happened between you two, but you'd better not let that girl get away this time."

"Corra, she lives in Chicago. What do you suggest I do?"

"I don't know, Rollin, but you'd better think of something. Tayler belongs in that house—I've seen it, I know it. And I know you've been thinking about closing down, but you can't. That's our legacy. Daddy saved all his life to buy that house. If I have to quit my job and start working there, I will. Just say the word."

He stood up. "Don't worry about the house. It'll be there. You get some rest." He fluffed her pillow and pulled the covers up on her.

Rollin sat back down as Corra finally succumbed to the drugs and stopped talking. Her eyelids fought a losing battle to stay open. He had never gotten around to talking to her about closing the B and B, but deep down, he'd known she wouldn't want him to close it. He watched her drift off to sleep.

He left to let Corra get some rest. On the ride home he thought about her dream, or vision, of Tayler holding a baby. Corra could have been talking out of her head since they had her all drugged up. He didn't know what to make of it, but Tayler had admitted she loved him, and he loved her, so now what? He wanted her to stay, but asking her to move to Danville from Chicago, and her agreeing, was a long shot.

Tayler and Kevin picked the kids up and drove them to the B and B for the night. Tayler put their belongings in the back bedroom she had vacated a week ago.

"Are you going to be okay?" Kevin asked.

"Yeah, I'm good. I'll get my things from Corra's tomorrow."

"Man, can you believe those guys walked away? You know it's usually the drunk driver that walks away and everybody else dies."

Tayler really didn't need to hear that right now.

"I probably shouldn't have said that last part, huh?" he added.

She shook her head. "Don't worry about it. You're right, though. I see it on the news all the time."

"Yeah, well, I still shouldn't have said it." He stood up. "I guess I'll go, if you're okay."

"I am, and thanks for everything today."

"Not a problem," he said, walking out of the kitchen.

Jamie and Katie darted past him, running down the hall.

"So, how much longer are you going to be in town?" he asked, dodging the kids.

She shrugged. "I'm not sure yet."

He played with his keys. "Yeah, I'm gonna hate to see you go. I looked forward to our morning rides. You're good company."

"Thanks Kevin. I miss them, too."

He blushed. "Maybe we'll get another morning in before you leave, right?"

"Maybe."

"We'll make the best of it, if so."

Tayler let Kevin out and went into Rollin's bedroom and exchanged her gown for a pair of sweatpants and a shirt that wasn't extremely big on her, then returned to the kitchen.

For once the house wasn't quiet. Jamie and Katie had pulled out one of the board games in the library and turned on the radio. Tayler welcomed the noise. It was past everyone's bedtime, but considering the situation, she let the kids stay up until Rollin returned.

She decided to surprise Rollin and have dinner ready when he walked in. Tonight he'd sample her cooking skills for the first time. Before she could finish dinner preparations, the back door opened and Rollin walked in. His shirt was pulled out of his pants and his tie hung loose. Tayler smiled at him, needing to see those big dimples to know that everything was okay.

He smiled. "How you doin'?"

She nodded. "I'm good. I thought I'd fix us some dinner," she said, pointing to the mess behind her.

He sighed. "You didn't have to do that. I'd have gone out to get some chicken or something."

"At this hour? Everything's probably closed. How's Corra?"

"She came through surgery with flying colors.

She's out like a light now." He walked over to her, cupped the side of her face in his palm and kissed her softly on the lips.

He caught her hand as she brought it up and kissed her knuckles.

"Uncle Rollin, where's Mama?"

They turned to see Katie standing in the entrance. Jamie stood behind her.

"I'll have dinner ready in a few minutes—why don't you guys go talk," Tayler said.

Rollin let go of Tayler's hand and went to them. He looked back over his shoulder. "We'll be in the library if you need some help."

"I've got it."

Tayler whipped everything together in no time then set the table. She could hear laughter from across the hall as Rollin played a game with the kids. She had to admit it sounded good. She felt like a mother and it was her family in the other room waiting on her to call them to dinner. This was the kind of family life she'd always dreamed of but never had.

When she walked into the library to let them know dinner was ready, all three of them were sitting on the floor working a puzzle.

"Dinner's ready."

The kids jumped up and ran to the dining room table.

"Hey, go wash your hands," Rollin said.

They changed directions and ran off to the bathroom.

"Sorry about that," he said.

"Don't worry about it. I'm enjoying them so much. I just hope they like dinner."

He walked over to Tayler and caressed her cheek with the back of his hand. "You look good in my sweats."

She laughed as he wrapped his arms around her and kissed her earlobe.

After dinner, Rollin put the kids to bed while Tayler cleaned up the kitchen. She waited around for him, but after almost twenty minutes she decided to retire to the library and listen to a little music.

Thirty minutes later, Rollin walked in.

"Here you are. I'm sorry I took so long. They wanted a bedtime story, and of course I didn't know any, so I had to make something up."

She laughed. "Oh, no, what kind of story did you come up with?"

He came over and sat down beside her. "I don't know, something about a little girl going to visit her grandmother and running from a big bad wolf."

"You're kidding? *Little Red Riding Hood*?"

He shrugged. "It's the only one I partially remember, and it did the trick. They nodded off before I could finish." He put his feet up on the coffee table and leaned back onto the couch. "Thank God we don't have any guests right now."

"Yeah." She joined him and laid her head back on the couch. "Rollin, I hope you aren't still considering closing the B and B. I think it's a lovely house, and you, Rita and Kevin are a great team."

He took a deep breath. "Corra talked to me about that tonight. I know I make it sound like it's all about money, but there's more to it than that."

"Do you mind telling me what? Because I told you about all the potential I see here."

He sat up and rubbed his palms down the front of his slacks. "Every time I have a house full of guests, I think about my mother all day. She loved this place full of people lounging in the library and sitting in the gardens. She lived to wake up and fix breakfast for a house full of people. It's hard to get over her death when I keep doing things that remind me of her."

"Even if you closed it, you would still live here, wouldn't you?"

"Yeah, I'm not letting go of the house. One time I thought about letting Corra and the kids move in, but then I'd have to buy another place and I can't afford to do that. Besides, she's never liked living out here."

"It's nice and quiet. I like it. But I see why it can be painful for you."

"Tonight with the kids running around, and you in the kitchen, it kind of reminded me of what the house used to be like when I was growing up."

"Rollin, you won't ever be able to escape the memory of your mother and father, and you shouldn't want to. It doesn't have to be painful, though. You've improved on the farm in your father's memory, and improving on the B and B will pay homage to your mother. Neither of those should be painful."

"Do you really like this place?" he asked.

"I love it here. You've seen how I've gone from not being comfortable in someone else's home to acting like I live here." She laughed.

"Which brings us to another subject," he said. He placed his arm around her shoulder and pulled her close to him. "Didn't you say something earlier about being in love with the proprietor of this little B and B?"

"I did, and I faintly remember a certain farmer admitting he was in love with me, too."

"I am. So, what do we do about that?" he asked.

"We make love," she said and pulled out of his embrace to turn around and kiss him.

Chapter 21

"The kids are asleep," he whispered.

"Yeah, in the room next to yours," she whispered back.

"But not next to yours."

Tayler pulled back and met his gaze. "I don't have a room here anymore, do I?"

"Upstairs, first room on the left."

"What if the kids come looking for you?"

"They won't." He kissed her forehead. "I want to make love to you tonight. I miss you. Can you understand that?"

"Yes, I've missed you, too."

Holding her hand, he stood up and brought her to her feet. He turned off the lights as they left the library but stopped before going upstairs.

"Wait a minute. I'll be right back." He dashed down

the hall to check on the kids and grab something from his room before he returned seconds later.

Tayler took his hand and they walked upstairs to the room she'd occupied for weeks. He opened the door and followed her inside. He didn't know if tonight would be their last night together or not.

He closed and locked the door behind him. Before his eyes stood a perfect, beautiful and intelligent woman that he thanked God for allowing him the pleasure of having. A chill ran through him when he thought about how badly he needed to hold her.

He walked over and took her face in the palm of his hands. "I love everything about you," he whispered.

"You don't know everything about me," she said in response.

"Then tell me. Tell me everything tonight. I want to know what makes you happy," he said and kissed the tip of her nose.

"That does."

"What makes you sad?" he asked and kissed her on the lips.

She poked out her bottom lip. "Having to leave you."

"What did you look like in elementary school? Did you wear braces, or glasses, or both?"

She started laughing.

"I want to know what, more than anything, gives you the most pleasure in life."

"Being right here with you in your arms," she whispered.

He slid one hand up the nape of her neck and pulled her mouth to his and kissed it.

"I also want to know what causes you the most

pain." He bit her bottom lip and sucked it into his mouth before kissing her again. He pulled back when he felt a tear roll down from her cheek onto their lips.

"The thought of having to leave you causes me more pain than you will ever imagine," she whispered.

He wiped away the tears with the pad of his thumb and she wrapped her arms around his neck before offering him her mouth. They played a long and slow game of exploration until he wanted to explode.

She kissed him with an urgency that said she was ready to make love. If tonight was their last night together, he wanted to make it memorable.

Tayler held onto Rollin as he lifted her into his arms, with her legs wrapped around him, and carried her over to the bed. He lowered her onto her back and leaned over to plant a soft kiss on her forehead.

She loved the way he held her as if she was light as a feather. She wanted him to caress her all over in that delicate way of his. No man had ever made her feel so wanted or special before.

"Look at them lips," he said before covering her mouth again. "I can't get enough of you."

Her body ignited at his touch. She returned the kiss, raising her head to meet his.

Every time his hands touched her skin, a shiver ran through her body. When Rollin's fingers found their way under his shirt, she held her arms up until he slipped it over her head.

He slid his sweats over her hips with ease. She had on black string bikini panties. He traced the hem of her underwear before pulling them past her hips and onto the floor.

He backed up and stared down at her as though he was taking a picture with his mind. One he never wanted to forget. She loved the longing way he stared at her, making her feel sexy.

"You are so beautiful—did I ever tell you that?"

She giggled. "I don't mind you telling me again, and again, and again."

"You are the most beautiful woman I've ever met, hands down. And I'm not just talking about your body. Baby, I love everything about you."

"Even my prissy little ass?" she asked rolling her eyes.

He grabbed her butt with both hands and squeezed. "Especially your prissy little ass."

He unbuttoned his white dress shirt. Underneath he had on a white T-shirt. Tayler helped him out of the dress shirt before she pulled his T-shirt out of his slacks and over his head.

His body was so finely chiseled she couldn't stop herself from leaning forward and kissing the center of his chest. He stopped unbuckling his belt and let her kiss him before pulling her up to taste her mouth again.

Her body was on fire and brimming with anticipation for what was sure to be the new best night of her life. She pushed her tongue into his mouth and clung to him like a woman desperate to be satisfied. He reached down and wrapped his arms around her body, repositioning her on the bed. When he let her go, she was dizzy and thought she might faint. She shivered from the coolness of the room.

"Are you cold?" he asked.

"I'm actually burning up, only from the inside out."

He smiled down at her and unzipped his pants.

Before he dropped them on the floor he removed a condom from his back pocket and pitched it onto the nightstand. "Then let me see if I can put that fire out."

As he stepped out of his shoes, she slid, naked, back onto the bed until she reached the bedspread and pulled it down underneath her.

If she was an artist she'd want to paint him. She wanted a photograph or something to help her remember him always.

Then he slid out of his briefs and came for her. She spread her legs as his hairy thighs settled against hers, sending a tingling sensation throughout her body. She pulled him around the waist, wanting to feel him closer against her skin. His broad shoulders and firm chest leaned over her as his mouth dipped down and captured one of her nipples. His hot mouth caused her to arch her back and let him feed on her breasts, one at a time.

She caressed his head with both hands and felt him suckling down to her toes. How this man excited her.

"Your breasts are perfect. Did I ever tell you that you have the prettiest breasts in the world?" He leaned over and flicked her nipple with his tongue.

She groaned and contracted her pelvic muscles while trying to keep her cool. "How would you know? Have you seen all the breasts in the world?"

"Nope, just my share. But these are perfect for me. They fit my hand," he said as caressed one breast. "And they fit my mouth," he added before bending over and sucking one breast into his mouth.

She'd fantasized all week about making love to him again. Her legs began to tremble when her hands moved down his stomach between his legs to caress him. He was hard and enormous in her hands. She needed to feel him inside her.

He groaned from her touch and released her breasts to look down at her caressing him. He watched her stroke him and then looked up into her eyes. Tayler bit her lip as he reached over to the nightstand and grabbed a condom. While he opened the wrapper she opened her legs wider, needing to feel all of him inside her. He clasped his hand over hers to stop her.

"Hold on, baby." His fingers had found their way between her legs, where he caressed and stroked her with two fingers.

"You're so wet," he whispered.

"You do this to me."

He thrust his fingers deeper inside her and she let go of him and came up off the bed. When she came down, she grabbed his shoulders and pulled him closer to her. Her body quivered from a deep need for him.

He rose onto one hand and loomed over her, looking down into her eyes. He withdrew his fingers and spread her thighs wide. She opened up like a blooming flower for him. At first, he slid inside her slowly. Then he pulled out and went back in, this time stretching her a little more. She relaxed every muscle in her body until he'd filled her with himself and started thrusting in and out of her. She moaned from the sheer pleasure of being filled to capacity with him.

After a few seconds, he slid out of her and back in, harder this time. She moaned louder.

"Shh." He bent down to cover her mouth with his. She wrapped her arms around him and held on for dear life. He thrust his love inside her with such intensity that she met him thrust for thrust and wrapped one leg around him, not wanting him to leave her. The body heat between them grew until it reached inferno status.

Rollin reached back for her leg and held it up as high as he could, allowing him to lay his love deeper inside her.

Tayler couldn't catch her breath.

He grunted again as he found his way even deeper inside her. In a nice and slow rhythm he worked himself in and out of her until Tayler thought she would scream. She reached down and grabbed the sheet, clutching it between her balled fists.

He leaned over and massaged her breasts until she started to throw her head from side to side. His hand slid down over her sweat-soaked chest and stomach until his fingers played in her hair.

The sensation inside her was building and almost bubbled over when he found her clitoris and positioned his thumb, then massaged her into an absolute frenzy. His thrusts increased as he now hammered in and out of her, looking down at her body with hooded eyes and his mouth wide-open, as though he couldn't catch his breath, either.

Tayler grabbed the pillow and bit down into it when the volcano inside her began to erupt. He moved his hand and groaned as he ground his release into her, letting go of her leg. Their bodies shook together as they gasped for air until their bodies went limp.

It took a few minutes for Tayler's breath to steady and her head to stop spinning. She lay there with Rollin's sweat-soaked body pressed against her. His hard body almost cut off her breathing.

"Rollin," she whispered, because that's all she could do.

He slowly rose up on one elbow and looked at her.

"I can't breathe."

He smiled and eased off her.

"Wait a minute." She grabbed him by the butt, not letting him pull out of her. She closed her eyes. "Not just yet."

"Baby, you might want to rethink that and give me a minute."

She laughed and let go. He rolled over onto his back.

"Whew," he exhaled. Without saying a word he quickly went to dispose of the condom, then returned to lay next to her.

She rolled over, kissed his chest and then laid her head on his chest. "I have a confession to make."

"What's that?" he asked.

"Sex with you is better than butter-pecan ice cream."

"Tell me you really like butter-pecan ice cream."

She rose on one elbow. "It's my favorite thing in the world."

He wrapped his arm around her and pulled her up to kiss her lips. "You are the most amazing woman I've ever met."

"I know," she said and laid her head back on his chest. She marveled in the moment, not wanting to leave his side. His chest rose and fell as his breathing settled to a steady pace.

"So, now what do we do? I don't want to let you go—you know that, don't you," he confessed.

"Sleep up here tonight," she suggested.

"That's not what I meant."

Rollin sat up and pulled her with him until they were propped up against the headboard. "Are you going back to work on the conference with Nicole?"

"I was wondering if you cared or not."

"Of course I care. I never wanted you to leave in the first place. I thought we had something too special to let go. I mean, I can't do anything but accept it if you go, but—"

She pulled out of his arms and turned in the bed to face him. "Rollin, are you trying to ask me to stay?"

He took a deep breath and reached out to caress her face. "The one thing I want more than anything in this world is for you to stay here with me, but not just until your vacation's over. I want more than that."

He looked so vulnerable at the moment, as if he was pleading with her.

"I need your love, and I'll love you like you've never been loved before. You already know I can provide a good home for you. And you did say you liked the B and B. Do you think you could live here in the B and B?"

Her heart overflowed with so much emotion, tears welled in her eyes. She couldn't stop them from overflowing. She sniffled and pulled herself together.

"Before I left Chicago, I already worked out a replacement for the conference."

He blinked. "You did?"

"Yeah, you know why?"

He took a deep breath and shook his head.

"Because I don't want to get back into that rat race. But more importantly, I met this great guy and fell head over heels in love with him. The only problem is I haven't known him very long."

"How is that a problem?"

"I don't know if he wants the same things out of life that I do."

"I want a family. I want a wife that loves me and has my back at all times. I want a woman that drives me crazy in bed. And someone I can grow old with. That's what I want out of life. How about you?"

She traced her finger along his chest. "I want a man that will love me endlessly. A man that won't cheat on me, or put me down, but lift me up. Somebody I can walk beside and not behind. And, last but not least, someone that makes me feel like the sexiest woman in the world when we make love."

"Do I do that?" he asked.

She nodded. "You take me to a place I've never been before, and I want to stay there."

"It sounds like we're made for each other. If you think you can leave the Windy City behind and call Coleman House home, we can work on getting to know each other better."

"I don't just think I can. I know I can." Tayler wanted to burst, she was filled with so much excitement.

He smiled so hard she leaned over and kissed his dimples. They held onto each other not wanting to let go—ever.

Chapter 22

The next morning, Rollin ran by Corra's to get Tayler's overnight bag. After a late breakfast, Rollin, Tayler and the kids hopped into Rollin's truck and headed for the hospital. When they walked into Corra's room, Rita, Wallace and Chris were there visiting.

The kids made a beeline for their mother, hugging and smothering her with kisses. Jamie wanted to see her cast.

Rollin pulled the only other empty chair in the room over for Tayler to sit down. Chris walked over to Rollin and shook hands.

"Can I write my name on your cast?" Jamie asked his mother.

"Sure, baby. Does somebody have a pen?"

Rita produced one.

"Did they behave last night?" Corra asked Rollin.

"Of course they did. You know they don't ever give Uncle Rollin any trouble, do you?" he asked the kids.

Katie giggled and shook her head. Jamie was busy scribbling his name on his mother's cast.

"Rollin, I missed you in church this morning," Rita said.

He turned from Chris and nodded. "I know. After last night, I kind of overslept." He glanced at Tayler.

"You need to make sure you don't miss next Sunday, and bring Tayler."

All eyes were on her. She smiled. "I'd love to go."

"Will you be here next Sunday?" Corra asked.

Tayler smiled up at Rollin. "I sure will."

"So, you're not going back to help Nicole with that conference?" Corra asked.

"What conference?" Chris asked.

Corra shushed him and looked from Tayler to Rollin.

"No, we managed to work something out."

"Why are y'all in that girl's business this morning?" Wallace asked.

Rita turned and gave him a stern look. "Wallace, why don't you go find me some coffee."

He walked away from her and over to join the other men in the room. "You already had one cup too many this morning. I'm not going anywhere. I want to know if Rollin asked her to stay or not, too."

All eyes turned to Tayler, except the kids'.

She smiled and cleared her throat.

"I'll be going back to Chicago at the end of the month," Tayler announced.

Corra looked up with a sad face then turned evil eyes at Rollin. "I'm sorry to hear that."

"So am I," Rita added and joined Corra in glaring at Rollin.

"Oh, I'll only be there long enough to settle some affairs and put my condo up for sale."

"I knew it," Wallace shouted and walked over to Rollin. "Boy, you've got a good head on your shoulder after all. I told you not to let this pretty little thing get away."

The room suddenly filled with chatter as everyone wanted to know what Rollin had said to convince her to stay. Corra motioned for Tayler to come closer and give her a big hug. Which she did, and then Rita had to have one.

"So, what did he say to get you to give up life in the big city?" Corra asked.

"Corra, mind your business," Rollin teased.

"This is my business. You're my brother."

Tayler walked over to Rollin and put her arm around his waist, and he held onto her.

"He promised me something I haven't had in a long time. A family."

* * * * *

Reunion in
paradise

Grace Octavia

Under the Bali Moon

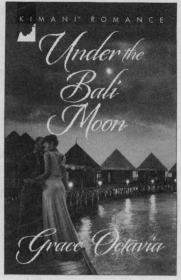

Ambitious attorney Zena Shaw loves her younger sister too much to watch her rush into a marriage she'll later regret. So she plans to prevent the nuptials in exotic Bali. But Zena's mission hits an obstacle in the form of gorgeous Adan Peters, who now regrets once breaking Zena's heart. From stunning beaches to magnificent temples, he'll show her everything this lush island has to offer—and hope these magical nights are only the beginning of forever…

Available May 2016!

www.Harlequin.com

Second-chance romance

AlTonya Washington

KIMANI™ ROMANCE

Provocative
ATTRACTION

AlTonya Washington

Provocative
ATTRACTION

Viva Hail always dreamed of a world far away from her Philadelphia roots, and it cost her the man she loved. Now Rook Lourdess is back in her life. As her personal bodyguard, the world-renowned security expert sweeps her off to his chalet in Italy, rekindling a desire that could forgive the mistakes of the past. Will their reignited passion offer a chance to write a new ending, or is Rook giving in to a temptation that could break his heart once again?

Available May 2016!

HARLEQUIN®
™ www.Harlequin.com

KPAW4510516

REQUEST YOUR FREE BOOKS!

2 FREE NOVELS PLUS 2 FREE GIFTS!

KIMANI ROMANCE™

Love's ultimate destination!

YES! Please send me 2 FREE Harlequin® Kimani™ Romance novels and my 2 FREE gifts (gifts are worth about $10). After receiving them, if I don't wish to receive any more books, I can return the shipping statement marked "cancel." If I don't cancel, I will receive 4 brand-new novels every month and be billed just $5.44 per book in the U.S. or $5.99 per book in Canada. That's a savings of at least 16% off the cover price. It's quite a bargain! Shipping and handling is just 50¢ per book in the U.S. and 75¢ per book in Canada.* I understand that accepting the 2 free books and gifts places me under no obligation to buy anything. I can always return a shipment and cancel at any time. Even if I never buy another book, the two free books and gifts are mine to keep forever.

168/368 XDN GH4P

Name _____ (PLEASE PRINT)

Address _____ Apt. # _____

City _____ State/Prov. _____ Zip/Postal Code _____

Signature (if under 18, a parent or guardian must sign)

Mail to the **Reader Service:**

IN U.S.A.: P.O. Box 1867, Buffalo, NY 14240-1867
IN CANADA: P.O. Box 609, Fort Erie, Ontario L2A 5X3

**Want to try two free books from another line?
Call 1-800-873-8635 or visit www.ReaderService.com.**

* Terms and prices subject to change without notice. Prices do not include applicable taxes. Sales tax applicable in N.Y. Canadian residents will be charged applicable taxes. Offer not valid in Quebec. This offer is limited to one order per household. Not valid for current subscribers to Harlequin® Kimani™ Romance books. All orders subject to credit approval. Credit or debit balances in a customer's account(s) may be offset by any other outstanding balance owed by or to the customer. Please allow 4 to 6 weeks for delivery. Offer available while quantities last.

Your Privacy—The Reader Service is committed to protecting your privacy. Our Privacy Policy is available online at www.ReaderService.com or upon request from the Reader Service.

We make a portion of our mailing list available to reputable third parties that offer products we believe may interest you. If you prefer that we not exchange your name with third parties, or if you wish to clarify or modify your communication preferences, please visit us at www.ReaderService.com/consumerschoice or write to us at Reader Service Preference Service, P.O. Box 9062, Buffalo, NY 14240-9062. Include your complete name and address.

KROM15

THE WORLD IS BETTER WITH

Romance

Harlequin has everything from contemporary, passionate and heartwarming to suspenseful and inspirational stories.

Whatever your mood, we have a romance just for you!

Connect with us to find your next great read, special offers and more.

f /HarlequinBooks

🐦 @HarlequinBooks

www.HarlequinBlog.com

www.Harlequin.com/Newsletters

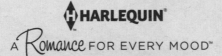

⬥HARLEQUIN®

A *Romance* FOR EVERY MOOD™

www.Harlequin.com

SERIESHALOAD2015